Which Path You Take

Books in The Looking Glass Saga:

Return to Womderland

Jabberwocky's Book

Borrowed, Not Lost

Wandering Hearts

Paint the Roses Red

Beauty Sleep

Which Path You Take

LOOKING GLASS SAGA

BOOK SEVEN

Which Path You Take

TANYA LISLE

SCRAP PAPER ENTERTAINMENT

Scrap Paper Entertainment
www.scrappaperentertainment.com

Contents

Chapter 1

HER GRADES MAY have been subpar, but Alice was not grounded. It was a surprise when she found the door unlocked the next day, but she soon found out why. Her father had been upset that she hadn't done any of the cleaning around the house when he came home, didn't have dinner ready, and the bedrooms were not adequately cleaned.

After vacuuming under her bed, Alice was very careful to never mention Ms. Miller. She never appeared and her father never mentioned her in the same way that he never mentioned her mother or her sister. Where there was once a rope that she could use to escape, there was now nothing at all. They had been found out and Ms. Miller would never be seen again.

At least there was a good deal of solitude. Even with the cameras watching her, there were plenty of places she could hide from them when she was overwhelmed. It gave her time to process what had happened. She had known for so long that she wasn't going to make it to high school, but here she was and she didn't know what to think.

The tears would hit her at random times during the day when her mind wandered to absolutely anything if she was not careful. She'd won the bet, whether she intended to or not. She was alive, and she would have to continue, and that was supposed to be a good thing. There was nothing for her to be sad about. She didn't know what was doing it.

That was a lie. She knew what it was. But she avoided the mirrors and tried not to think about it.

Spending so much time in Wonderland was a mistake. It had been a month of freedom, of not worrying about what she had left behind or what she would have to go back to. They raided the castle and recovered a great many hearts, as well as set the queen's army back in numbers. Alice even managed to have tea at a tea party.

But she couldn't put any of the hearts back. She tried so hard all month, but not one would go back in place. The one thing Wonderland needed her to do, and there was no way for her to do it anymore.

It was better that she wasn't there. Best not to give them hope and invite their ire when she couldn't deliver.

Still, she would have to go back to Wonderland someday to help repair the damage or it would come for her. Already, she could see Wonderland even in the reflection of the pot as she boiled spaghetti, tempting her to return. Neverland remained a looming threat, still seeping into Wonderland and causing more problems the longer that hole remained between the worlds.

And there was school. Eventually, she would be sent back to deal with the grades that the Bandersnatch had left her. They were lower than her father preferred, but those would be easy enough to bring back up so long as she focused. The larger issue was trying to repair the relationships she had left broken and she didn't know where to begin with that. It was probably best to figure it out with Adrianna. She would know what to do and if there was anything left there to salvage.

And then there was Sarah. She had noticed that Alice took her time returning, had been aware of just how long she was gone. Sarah had hugged her so tight when she came back and looked so happy that she hadn't been taken away by the Bandersnatch forever. The reminder that someone knew she was gone at all and had remembered even after her time away…

Her emotions rose in her throat again. She checked the time, seeing it was almost seven already. With a deep, steadying breath, she drained the pasta and turned off the elements on the stove, forcing her hands to remain steady as she took out two plates to prepare. Her father might be home soon, and she was not going to be caught crying. He would not like that.

Alice picked up her book and took a seat on the couch, listening carefully for the front door as she opened her book. It looked like a history book on World Wars, but inside was a novel that Ms. Miller had left behind for her before she was banished. The books never talked back, but they spoke to her in ways that she needed, bringing her away from her thoughts and showing her how other people were dealing with their less than ideal situations.

"A treacle is not meant to be caged. No matter how rude it may be when it cannot do its duty."

Alice blinked hard at the page and refused to look up. Instead, she let out a sigh and forced any wandering thoughts away. Sometimes when she was reading, she could almost hear Wonderland, and that was particularly bad when she knew her father would be home soon.

She checked the time again. It had been half an hour and her father had not made it home yet. She put the book aside and went to make herself a plate. If he was not home by now, he likely wouldn't be home at all. With care to make sure she didn't spill anything onto the clean counters, she created a plate for herself.

She made it all the way to the counter with her plate before she heard the front door open, then brought it to the dining room to set it down in her father's spot before going to make herself another. When she returned to the dining room, her father was already sitting with a fork in hand and inspecting the noodles as Alice took her seat beside him. He looked up and regarded her, a frown on his face.

Something was coming.

"There will be a technician coming tomorrow," he told her. "Let him in. The new ones aren't working properly."

"Okay," she said, waiting. She could feel her father watching her and she took a small bite. At least he couldn't be mad about the food.

"You've spent far too much of your day crying instead of studying," he told her. "Instead of feeling sorry for yourself, you should be working on raising those grades. No one wants to marry an idiot."

Alice went very still, her mind circling over what he'd just said. She had not shed a tear when her father was around. She was very careful about that. She hid from the cameras when she did cry, so he had no way to know what she was doing when he wasn't there.

He let out a small laugh and she wouldn't look at him. "You didn't even notice, did you?" he asked. "Had to make sure your mother wasn't trying to get away with anything else, so I had to get a few extra cameras installed. She thought she was so clever. Can't let that woman get an inch or she thinks she can get away with anything. And now I know how upset my daughter has been because she had her precious phone taken away. Maybe if you had paid better attention in school, I would have let you keep it. You'll have to behave yourself if you want it back at all."

There were more cameras in the house. She didn't even have to question it. She knew it was a possibility and had no doubts that her father would have done it. There were times when she might have wondered if he was really watching them carefully, that she had acted mostly just to be safe, but now she knew he was actively monitoring them. And he had seen her.

It wasn't just the tears he might have seen. He might have seen her disappearing around the house. Might have seen her checking under the covers of her supposed textbooks to find out what she was really reading. Might have seen flashes of Wonderland in the reflections she walked past. He might have seen everything he needed to send her away.

"It's about time you started attending church," he told her. "You'll be coming on Sunday. Some good young men there might be a better influence on you. Your mother didn't think it was a good idea, but…"

Alice nodded. She wasn't listening anymore, thinking only of the cameras. She resisted the urge to look around, to try to find them all. Her father would know if she was looking for them tomorrow. He would see her doing so and that would make him angry. Could she follow the technician around and see if he could show her where they were? She needed to find blind spots, but didn't know how without knowing where the cameras might be.

"Are you listening, Alice?"

She hadn't heard a thing, but her mouth moved anyway. "We'll be having people over on Saturday."

He looked at her, appraising her once more, and Alice forced her panicked thoughts away. She had to think only of right here and right now. Her father already looked displeased and she couldn't do anything to make that worse.

"I'll be expecting you to be on your best behaviour," he continued. "I've been lenient so far, but if you do anything to embarrass me, you won't be going back to that school of yours in September. Do you understand?"

The bottom dropped out of her stomach. There wasn't a doubt in her mind that he would do it. "Yes," Alice said.

He looked pleased by that and went back to dinner. Alice, despite having lost her appetite, forced herself to continue in silence. Her father continued to talk, to tell her what he expected from her moving forward, and Alice did her best to keep her eyes from scouring every corner of the house for the new cameras that now watched her every move.

CHAPTER 2

New Outlook

THE SUMMER WAS passing by too fast. From Ryan, her oldest brother, announcing that he was engaged, to Evan getting into law school, they had a lot to celebrate and things to do. At least Ryan wasn't getting married until next summer, though Adrianna couldn't really imagine much changing once he was. There was already talk of how they would make a wedding happen.

Not that she wasn't keeping in touch with everyone else. She got to see what all of her friends were up to all summer, seeing a stream of photos along with a group chat for commentary about what was going on. Kevin had nearly gotten another brother named John, a boy that Sarah seemed more interested in than Adrianna expected for someone she had never met. Rob was going to a gaming conference to meet with people who were interested in his game. Sarah and

Heather were not quiet, but their summers largely were and they spent more time asking about the wedding than anything else.

But as she looked through the messages on her phone, she knew there was one who had not said a word to her since the start of the summer.

"Alice hasn't said anything all summer," Adrianna said, putting her phone back down. Rayne had Adrianna's basket of laundry in hand, still working part time as a maid in their house to help with the chores so she could pay for her schooling. It was nice to see her still there, even if she was there to work. She looked a little like Alice, even with the short blue hair, and clipped her vowels in the same way she did. It was selfish, she knew, but Rayne's every word clarified that she was a very different person from Alice.

"Oh, she's not keeping her phone," Rayne told her, a humourless laugh escaping her lips and the smile on her lips entirely sarcastic. She looked at Adrianna and let her shoulders drop, putting the laundry back down and sitting on the end of her bed. "You can blame me for that. I got to keep my phone and the internet and I turned out gay. Dear old Dad is *not* making that mistake twice."

"You think she's okay?"

It looked like Rayne was thinking about lying to her. She didn't look away as she spoke, though. "Alice can handle it," she said. "I don't know how much Mom could really do to stop him anyway, so it's probably not that much worse."

Rayne looked away at the end and Adrianna was worried. She didn't know how to ask what was wrong or why she looked so sad. Rayne covered it quickly, but Adrianna had seen it and decided that she would ask later when she wasn't trying to finish her job.

"Rayne!"

They both looked to the door, but no one was there yet. "What?" Rayne called back.

"Your mom's on the phone!" The voice, Adam, was closer now.

"Give me a minute!" Rayne called back, getting up and looking at her cell. "Oh, whoops," she said, looking at the screen. She pulled a face and hurried out the door, disappearing down the hall to the closest phone.

Adrianna got up and went the other way toward the kitchen, finding Adam waiting at the top of the steps, his eyes lingering on a mirror in the hall. He'd been doing that more and more lately, watching the mirrors like he expected them to do something. He was never staring at himself but waiting for them to show him something he would rather see.

"Hey?" she asked as she got closer to him. "Are you okay?"

"Yeah," Adam said, though he didn't stop staring at the mirror.

"You wanna eat something?"

"Sure."

Adrianna gently eased him away from the mirror and downstairs. It felt like everyone around her was obsessed with Wonderland. "What was it like in Wonderland?" she asked as she guided him back down the stairs. Slowly he was coming back to himself again, and he had been angry when he wasn't properly distracted. Lance said talking about Wonderland usually made him feel better.

"I should be there," he said. "Alice won't commit to saving it. She had no right to keep me from doing *her* damn job."

Lance hadn't warned her of the malice and the ire that came with Adam's words, but she wasn't surprised. "We're happy you're back," she told him. "We were worried when you disappeared."

Adam stopped just outside of the kitchen and looked at her, eyes narrowed. "Like Matt, right?" he asked.

"He'll be back," Adrianna assured him.

It was clear that Adam had other thoughts about that, but he said nothing else before turning back to the kitchen. Adrianna followed him back in, letting the sounds of her family take over and wash away the concerns of the last five minutes. Lance continued to be much better at dealing with Adam than she was, and Adrianna watched them go.

Her phone vibrated and she pulled it out of her pocket,

finding a message from Sarah waiting for her. She pulled it out and leaned against the counter, hoping that it was nothing too urgent.

Sarah

How many Liddells do you think are in Seattle?

I talked mom into taking me to this thing tonight

And his name is Liddell

Addie

You're going to see Alice

Adrianna could hardly believe it. She thought she would have to wait and hope that Alice showed up at the start of September. She pushed off of the counter, eyes locked on the screen and watching as she saw Sarah was typing. Her feet took her to the couch and she dropped into the corner, though her attention was on what Sarah was telling her.

Sarah

Maybe

Moms just going so aunt barb doesn't hook up with some rando

AGAIN

But if I see Alice

I can ask why she hasn't said anything all summer

Addie

Rayne says she probably doesn't have her phone

Sarah

ALL SUMMER?

I'm getting to the bottom of this

No way she doesn't have a phone all summer

Or the internet

It's Seattle not Saturn

Adrianna felt light as she read through that. She hadn't felt heavy before, but it was like a weight had left and she was almost floating. Someone was going to check

If she was there. A haunting memory from years ago itched in the back of her mind, something she had said once. That she had not been allowed at the parties. But surely this time, surely now that she was older she wouldn't be locked away while her father had people over. Without her mother there to help, surely she would have to step in.

That made sense, right? But she had been warned that Mr. Liddell didn't always make sense.

Addie

She might be grounded. You might not see her

Sarah

If she's in that house I am finding her

She can't hide from me

;)

Adrianna smiled down at her phone. Finally, someone would check on her. Soon she would know. One less thing to be worried about. Now, if only Adam were that easy.

CHAPTER 3

The Party

ALICE HAD NEVER been allowed out of her room when her parents threw their parties before. She used to wonder about the sound of adults downstairs mulling about, the faint music playing that could just be heard under the conversation, and the laughter that always sounded just a little strange to her ears.

Now that she was here, she wasn't sure what else she expected. There were a lot of adults and very few people her own age who she could talk to. Not that she could really allow herself to have a conversation. Her father kept a careful eye on her, watching and waiting to see if she would do anything that might embarrass him. She was very careful to be on her best behaviour, saying only what was necessary and nothing more.

She felt like a pet. People kept asking her the same questions about school and she gave the same answers over and over again. She smiled and performed as best she could, but she found herself quickly drained as the night wore on. She knew better than to ask for the time, but thankfully others were quick to pull out their phones and she was not against catching a glimpse. It had barely been an hour into the evening and she already wanted it to be done.

"Alice!"

Though she couldn't see who had called for her, Alice was happy for the interruption, not sure how many times she could hear that people she had never met were so surprised to see her and how her father spoke well of her. It was tiresome, but she kept the plastic smile on her face, glancing over at her father as his eyes wandered elsewhere.

Sarah waved at her from only a short distance away and separated from the women she came in with. A blond and a brunette, both looking like they might have walked out of a magazine let her leave their company, the blonde holding the brunette back from wandering off herself.

Was she supposed to know that Sarah was here? Did her father know? Alice looked back, but he wasn't paying her any attention right now. Her eyes flicked up, looking for the cameras watching her every move. Even if he wasn't looking at her, he was always watching. And he would know if she was anything but happy to see her friend.

Alice couldn't read the expression on Sarah's face. There

was a mix of things there, most of them making Alice wary about how close she was getting. Indignation. Anger. Concern. Happiness even managed to shine through genuinely despite it all, and Alice didn't know how to react. What would look the most normal? She wasn't even sure if those cameras recorded her actions for her father to watch later, but she didn't want to risk it.

Sarah had braces. How long had she had braces?

"I didn't know you were coming," Alice said. "How are you?"

"Oh no, you don't get to do that," Sarah snapped at her. Her eyes were wide and suddenly Alice could tell very clearly that she was in trouble. "Where have you *been?* You haven't even *read* a message we've sent since the end of the year. And—"

Sarah caught herself, eyes going round and looking around before she looked back at Alice. She looked like she might say more, but she was flushing under the makeup she was wearing. "I need to talk to you in private."

"I…" Alice glanced back at her father. He was talking with the two women Sarah had come in with. The brunette was taking a particular interest.

Sarah glanced over at them and let out a click with her tongue. "Don't worry, Mom will make sure she doesn't do anything," she told her.

Panic welled up in her. This evening felt like a test, like her father was watching her to make sure she would do nothing out of line. Disappearing from his sight would surely make him mad, and he was already so tense. She didn't want to do anything that might make him decide she couldn't go back to school. "I can't..."

"Look," Sarah said, exasperated. "Is your dad rich?"

"I think so."

"Then she'll make sure he doesn't notice. Come on, we need to talk."

Sarah pulled them away, getting promptly lost as soon as they left the main room. Heart pounding, Alice led the way away from there and down the hall, skirting the sides and taking a very deliberate path through the back of the house. She hoped that they weren't recording her actions or she might get in trouble for this later.

"Is that a camera?" Sarah asked. Alice didn't say anything, continuing through the side of the house and onto the small landing outside the side door. She looked around and spotted a glare, one that might be another camera, and led her a little further away. It was dimly lit here, but it might be safe. She really hoped they didn't record anything.

"I just meant away from the party," Sarah told her. "We could have just gone to your room."

Alice shook her head. "This is safer if you want to talk about... that stuff."

"That..." Sarah looked at a loss for words. She looked back, scanning the spot they had been and squinting at the same glare Alice had noticed. Rounding back on Alice, Sarah shook her head and removed any control she had over her volume. "Where the *hell* have you been?" she demanded. "You've completely ghosted everyone since we left school! Even Addie can't get in touch with you!"

Somehow, the strangest part of that was that Sarah called her Addie. Was Alice supposed to do that too? It felt strange. "I'm sorry," Alice said, the response automatic.

"I don't want an *apology* Alice," Sarah said. "What *happened?* At the very least, you usually check messages, even if you don't say anything. Did you lose your phone or something? Change your number? *What?*"

Alice hesitated. She wasn't sure if she should say, but her father had never said not to. "I'll get it back when I start school again," she said. A look went across Sarah's face, and Alice added, "My computer too."

"So Addie was right," Sarah said finally. "*All summer* you've been offline."

Alice nodded. Sarah said nothing and the silence lingered between them, neither of them quite sure how to break it.

Thoughts came to Alice, questions now that she knew Sarah had been in touch with everyone. Regrets that she had, curiosities about what had happened. She had only really had a day of being at school before she went back home. And the last day she'd actually been there, Sarah made it clear that she knew that Alice hadn't been around.

"Is Heather still mad at me?" Alice asked.

Anything would have been better than what Sarah said.

"I can't believe you've just been offline." Sarah looked incredulous at her. Alice wondered if she'd actually heard her or not. "Have you talked to *anyone?* No, of course not, who else would you talk to?"

Alice was pretty sure she was supposed to be offended, but she stayed quiet. Sarah started to pace, to move a little too close to where the light was. Alice caught her by the wrist to stop her and Sarah snapped around, staring at her wide eyed. "What?" she demanded.

Alice's eyes flickered up to the camera, but the words died on her lips. She didn't have to worry about that right now. With any luck, they weren't recording. The technician didn't seem to think the new ones were, anyway, and they were far enough away from the old one. Not to mention Lance had reacted badly to the cameras when he found out about them. It was probably best not to mention that she was avoiding them.

Sarah followed Alice's eye and saw the camera. Her body

shifted, looking at it better as Alice let her go. "There's really cameras in your place everywhere, aren't there?" Sarah asked, sounding amazed. "Lance said something about them but no one believed him. There's cameras inside too, aren't there?"

Alice wouldn't look back at her. She could feel Sarah's eyes on her, hear that concern and judgement in her voice, and she wanted no part of it. "Dad's just really concerned about security," she said, the answer automatic. "It's not a big deal."

"I legit cannot believe Lance was telling the truth," Sarah said, looking back at Alice, though Alice didn't want to meet her eyes. "I mean, Addie talks to your sister, right? She lives there. And Addie said she said this was a thing, but I didn't think there were that many."

"It's not a big deal," Alice insisted, lowering her voice. They were outside and well away from prying ears, but everything Sarah said felt much too loud.

"This is nuts," Sarah told her. "Why don't you just disappear out of here? It's not like you can't."

"I can't just—"

Sarah rolled her eyes. "Of *course* you can. No one else remembers your trick that night, but I do. You could walk out of here and vanish into the night whenever you wanted. And a lot of other stuff. When you do, you can come stay with me, or we could get you across the country or something."

"I can't go," Alice said. She didn't want to tell Sarah anything more than that. She would take whatever Alice said and try to make it into a much bigger deal than it was. "Just... I can't leave. It's not so bad," Alice continued. She took a breath and finally looked Sarah in the eye. She was concerned, but there was so much judgement there. "Really. I'm doing fine. I'm just going to be offline until we get back to school."

"This is *insane*, Alice," Sarah insisted. "You need to get out of here. But first," she continued, fishing her phone out of her pocket. Quickly, she reached over and took a picture of the pair of them. Alice was too startled by the flash to smile, though Sarah didn't care as she started moving her fingers along the screen.

"What was that for?"

"So I can prove you're still alive," Sarah said, smiling. "Do you really have nothing? No phone, no computer? There has to be some way you can keep in touch with everyone."

"It's just one more week."

Sarah frowned, but her eyes traveled back into the house. "You're being called," she said quietly. "You need to go back, right?"

Alice nodded and took a step back toward the house. She could see her father in the window looking for her and her heart dropped. "Sorry, he probably needs me to..."

"I get it," Sarah said, something different in her tone as

they walked back to the house. "I'll be right here as long as you need me."

Alice could see her father in the window looking for her and felt her blood run cold in her veins. He was looking for her. Which meant he had noticed her missing. She couldn't have been gone for more than a couple minutes, and he was already looking out this far.

Sarah grabbed her hand and gave her a reassuring squeeze before pulling her back toward the house. Alice didn't try to pull away, walking a little faster to the house to make sure her father wouldn't be looking for too long. She can't have been gone for too long. And she was with a friend. He wouldn't blame her for Sarah's insistence, surely. At least, not until the party was over and she had time to come up with a reason.

They got in the house and Alice wasn't sure what to make of her father's new companion. He had traded Sarah's aunt for another woman. The dark hair and pale skin were far too familiar from her time at the Case's house and reminded her of the summer she could be having and hoped she could have again.

But what was Claudia doing here? Alice glanced around, but she saw no sign of any other members of Adrianna's family.

Claudia was the one whose eyes fell on her first, a smile

gracing her face and not looking at all bothered that Alice had been outside or that she had a friend with her.

"There she is," Claudia said, smiling at Alice. Her father didn't look like he cared one way or another what he was doing, at least not angry but not much of anything else either. "We've been looking for you, Alice. I wanted to have a word."

"Doesn't she look like Addie?" Sarah asked quietly as Alice pulled out of her grip.

With a breath to steel herself, Alice put her smile back on and went to join her father and Claudia. "Hello," Alice said, addressing her directly. She held out a hand to shake. "I didn't know you would be here."

Claudia smiled back at her and took the hand. Sarah stepped closer behind her, but Alice barely remembered she was there at all. "I thought I'd stop by. I have a favour to ask." Alice could feel a tingle spread up her arm that filled her head. Every hair on her scalp stood up on end, and that was the last she could remember of the evening.

CHAPTER 4

Status Report

IT WAS STRANGE enough that Sarah wanted to talk on camera, but it was even stranger that she insisted that Lance was there too. For all she insisted that she would explain when they were talking, Adrianna would rather she just *told* her what was going on. She already had to wait almost twelve hours since the photo for Sarah to tell her anything at all, and *She's alive and still Alice* didn't really help answer any of her questions about how she was doing.

She had seen the photo posted to the group chat. Alice looked fine, if confused. She still had those bags under her eyes like she hadn't been sleeping well, but she always looked somewhere between tired and exhausted. There was a party in the background and a shot of the house that Alice never talked about, the home she went back to that Rayne was so happy to be away from.

She wondered if she should get Rayne here as well, but Sarah was just coming online. Lance sat behind her on the bed, leaning into the frame and glancing at his phone as Sarah came on screen.

Sarah looked well rested, even without the makeup. At least, Adrianna thought there was none. She was never very good at telling. Her hair was tied loosely back in a braid that had gone its own way, but Sarah didn't seem to care about that at all as she stared at the screen, her lips moving with no sound coming out. She frowned, looking at something on her end. Her hands danced across the bottom of the screen before Adrianna heard the clicks of keys being hit.

"—now?" Sarah asked.

"We can hear you!" Adrianna said. "How was it?"

"Sorry, Addie, we'll get to that," she said quickly, her attention going over Adrianna's shoulder. "I got a problem with your brother to settle first."

"What?" Lance asked, looking up from his phone and at the screen. "Why me?"

"Why didn't you tell me about all those *cameras* everywhere?"

"What?" Lance repeated, trying to figure out what was going on. His phone went down on the bed as he crept closer to the camera to look at her. "Go back. What are we talking about?"

"At Alice's," Sarah repeated, though she was clearly losing her patience. "There were cameras *everywhere* in that place!"

"Oh," he said. "I mean, I didn't actually *see* any while I was there."

"How?"

Lance shrugged. "They aren't in her room. I left out the window and didn't see any."

"They're on the outside of her house too."

Lance shook his head. "I didn't see any. Alice just told me they were there."

Sarah fumed, but Adrianna could see that this wasn't going to get anywhere. She leaned into the frame in front of Lance. "How is she?" Adrianna asked.

Sarah looked like she had more to say to Lance, but she collected herself. She closed her eyes and took a deep breath, exhaling out and spreading her hands like she was getting rid of whatever else she wanted to say. "Alice," she said, "is alive."

The silence after the statement didn't help matters. It was clear that Sarah wasn't intending on continuing until she was asked more. "And?" Adrianna prodded.

"And," Sarah started, but then she held for a long pause. "And she needs to not be in that house."

"Did she mention the lock on her door?" Lance asked.

"He let her have a lock on her door?" Sarah looked surprised, but that soon melted away.

"It's on the outside."

"There we go."

"Is she okay?"

"She's…" Sarah kept pausing, like she was considering her words carefully. It was like she had a script in the back of her mind that she was trying to pull lines from. It was all carefully put, every word meticulously chosen. "She's doing the best she can. I will say that this helps explain her a lot. I get it now."

"What does that mean?"

"That she needs out of that house?" Lance offered.

"When she's ready," Sarah told him sharply. "But yeah. But she's okay," she added, her eyes going to a spot on the screen and staring intently. "She knows what she's doing, I think. She'll probably be okay. But she did disappear on me again. Even when you try to help that girl…"

"What do you mean, she disappeared?" Adrianna asked. That sounded exactly like her, but she didn't know what Sarah meant by it. Sarah didn't know that Alice could disappear, did she?

"Some woman wanted to talk to her and they wandered off without me. I didn't see her for almost an hour after I took that picture. When she showed up again, her dad was trying to get her to talk to some guy."

"What's her dad like?"

Sarah shrugged. "I didn't talk to him. He did keep trying to get Alice to talk to guys at the party, so that was weird. Aunt Barb liked him a little too much, though. Mom had to pry her off of him and we had to go early before she did something stupid. Which means he's probably an asshole."

"That's not—"

"Of course it's not," Sarah said swiftly, "Whatever you were going to say. Of course not. But Aunt Barb has *a type* and she has never gone wrong. Best asshole detector on the West Coast. If they hook up, we'll know for sure. Oh, I'll talk to you guys in a bit. I gotta go." Sarah said, turning back and away from the screen. Her hand came up over the camera and the screen tilted. She disappeared, the sound going off and the call disconnecting.

Lance let out a sigh and went back to his phone. "She didn't sound happy," he said.

Adrianna glanced down at his screen, seeing a string of messages with a lot of capital letters from the other person. She didn't manage to read any of them before Lance tilted the phone back to himself and started typing something else back. "Everything okay?" she asked.

Lance shrugged. "She can be mad if she wants," he said. "I told her there was something weird about that place. Not my fault no one believed me."

Adrianna closed her laptop and got up, putting it on her

desk. "Is it really that bad?" she asked. "Alice never really told me much about what it was like there. She just kind of changed the subject."

Lance looked down at his phone and frowned. "Can't just be one thing at a time," he muttered before letting out a breath and he looked at Adrianna. "She was grounded and that meant being locked in her room. Her tutor left the door unlocked, but she still wouldn't go out because she thought there were cameras that were going to watch her. Like, she knew where the blind spots were on the cameras. I didn't see any when I was leaving, but she said they were watching the outside of the house too. I don't know if they were really there, but she definitely thought they were."

Adrianna wrapped her arms around her, looking down at the corner of her bed. Lance picked his phone back up and started furiously messaging back as she let herself take a moment to process. She couldn't imagine her dad locking her in her room for anything, even if she was grounded. Lance had told her that Alice kept spare food in her desk in case her dad forgot to give her dinner, even. Alice had dismissed it, but now that she thought about it, that was horrifying. And she hadn't denied it.

Even Wonderland made some sense now. After what she was dealing with at home, Wonderland was...

No, it really wasn't worth it. It was an escape for her right now, and Adrianna couldn't fault her for that, but it would leave her eventually. She knew how stories like this ended, and how Alice's story with Wonderland had ended before. In the end, she would leave and she would never go back. She'd have to go back home. Back to that.

"Who are you talking to?" Adrianna asked absently as Lance's expression went from annoyed to relieved and his fingers relaxed around his phone.

"Rob," he said.

Adrianna narrowed her eyes on the phone. "Since when do you guys talk?"

"Game Club."

"Is everything okay?"

"Yep."

There were a lot of all caps messages for Rob to be okay, but she didn't press. She could find out her own way later if there was something wrong. She had more than enough on her mind, and Lance seemed to be handling whatever it was that was going on with him for now, at least. She was sure he'd talk about it in the group chat eventually.

"You don't believe me."

"Nope." Adrianna sat back down on her bed. "You're lucky I'm too worried about Alice."

"And changing my lock code…"

Adrianna shot him a glare, but he was already doing it.

That was fine. There were other ways to find out if she needed to, but that was definitely going to make it a bit harder.

Movement in the door caught her attention and she watched as Evan leaned in. "Do you guys know where Claudia went? Her office is completely empty."

Adrianna looked at him, eyes narrowed. "She left," she said. Evan should know that. They all knew that she was gone.

Evan watched her and waited for an elaboration that never came. "Is she coming back?"

"Nope," Lance said. Adrianna agreed.

There was a look that crossed over Evan's face, but he stayed very quiet. "Okay," he said, turning back and away. "Is Alice showing up this year?"

Adrianna shook her head. "Dad hasn't been able to get hold of her dad." Adrianna frowned, thinking of where she was now. "I don't know if he'll let her come anymore."

"Well, at least you're worried about that," Evan muttered as he backed out of the door.

She was missing something. "Did something happen?"

"Don't worry about it," he told her, waving as he left. "Not that you would."

Lance watched him go. "Something happened."

Adrianna dropped back on her bed, lying on her back with her arms stretched up to the pillow. "Why does it feel like everything's happening this summer?"

"Everything's always been happening Addie," Lance said, rapping his knuckles lightly on her forehead before getting up. She let out a small, irritated growl at him as she rubbed her forehead, but he didn't pay any attention. "You're just noticing now. Nice to have you back."

CHAPTER 5

Back to Normal

ALICE SAT IN the lobby of the high school dorms, waiting for them to get set up to give out the keys to her room for the rest of high school. The sun had only barely cracked across the horizon when she arrived, but her father was anxious to let her go. She was fine with it, especially since the building was unlocked and she had a place to sit with her suitcase. She put her feet on it, pushing it until it was stopped by the coffee table, and waited for the sun to rise properly as she started poking through her newly returned phone to see what remained.

Sarah had said they sent her messages throughout the summer, but there was nothing on her phone that implied she had received any of them. All of the apps that weren't essential to her phone had been removed, including Robert's game. Her father hadn't found a reason to scold her over anything on her phone or computer, so she assumed that her father hadn't found anything too objectionable in the technology. Not that she was particularly tech savvy.

Her computer was next and seemed to have a similar treatment. Things not related to school, and a few assignments that were, had been deleted. There were a few programs that she was pretty sure were meant to monitor her usage. She didn't try opening up any of the files in the parts of her hard drive that Lance assured her were hidden away, unsure of just what her father could see her doing on here now. She debated contacting some of her friends, to see if Lance had any idea what she should be doing, but his number was gone from her phone. The only one that remained was her father's, and he would not want to be bothered even if she did have anything to ask him.

Alice let out a sigh and looked out the window at the grounds. They looked like they were on fire, lit up in brilliant oranges and golds. It was pretty, but as she looked at it now, she thought she would have preferred sleep. Her head was throbbing just looking at the sunrise. A yawn escaped her, so insistent that her jaw cracked as it rushed out. She clapped her hands over her open mouth and jaw, eyes darting around for someone to apologize to, but she was alone. And she was still several hours away from anyone joining her.

Well. At least she could finish her book. Curling up in

the corner of the couch, she reached into her bag and pulled out a book with a cover insisting that it was about the biology of tree frogs. She was pretty sure tree frogs were on the menu in the post apocalypse that the characters were currently battling.

She hadn't heard anyone else come in, but something dark fell over her, casting a shadow over the pages. She looked up, finding that the daylight was now properly streaming in and there were a few people here now, milling about and looking like they were getting ready with the keys.

In front of her, Arthur was studying her and it looked like he was about to give her a failing grade. The summer had been kind enough to him. He took a seat across from her and leaned over the small coffee table between them, his long blond hair falling into his brown eyes. He looked like he'd gotten a lot more sleep than she had last night, at least, and he was already in his school uniform. Alice felt inappropriate dressed in her summer dress and cardigan. "Look who made it," he said. "You disappeared after that night."

"I graduated with everyone else," she said. Moving the slip of paper she was using as a bookmark into place, she shut the book and slipped it back into her bag. She didn't look away from Arthur, though he still didn't look satisfied.

Arthur rolled his eyes. His left hand tapped against the table, not moving and making a hollow sound with every strike. That was right. Wendy had removed that one. "You trapped me here and then you vanished. I didn't *ask* to come here."

"I'm not taking you back to Neverland."

Arthur looked like he might spit at the idea. "I am not going back to that hell."

"Then you're... fine?" She wasn't sure what he looked so irritated by.

"I've done what you want," he said, the last spoken word like a curse. "There's no reason to keep me here."

Alice shrugged. "You don't have to stay here," she said. "There's a lot of other schools you can go to."

"I'm not from this world, Liddell," he told her, his voice low.

"I'm not taking you back to Neverland."

"I'm not from that place."

"You make too much sense to be from Wonderland." Even so, he was giving her a headache.

Arthur flushed with anger and Alice shrank away from him, sinking deeper into the corner of the couch. She glanced back, reminding herself that there were people here. "I don't know where you're from," she said. "But if you tell me and I can figure out how to get there, I can try to take you back. I'll try."

A look crossed Arthur's face, one that Alice couldn't

read. There was some sadness there mixed in with anger and many other things that fought for dominance in his too sharp features and he rubbed at the place where his wrist met his prosthetic hand. "You have no idea who I am," he said, and in that Alice could hear the disdain. "Know that you brought me here, Liddell. And you're at fault for everything that happens next."

"Alice?" came a voice behind him. Alice looked back at the door and saw Robert making his way in, pulling a suitcase behind him with a backpack on his back.

Arthur vanished in front of her and Alice wondered if he had ever been there at all.

Robert sat down next to her on the couch, relaxing back into it for only a moment before leaning forward to take off his backpack and drop it on the floor. "Addie and the Cases are on the way. You been here long?"

"Nope," Alice said. At least if he didn't see Arthur, she didn't have to explain anything. "How was your summer?"

"Got more work done on that game," he said. "Calling it Clockpunk. What do you think?"

Behind him, people were starting to file in. She could see Adrianna and her brothers file in and she gave them a wave to let them know where they were. "I like it," she said, watching Adrianna veer off to where they were setting up to hand out keys. Alice tried not to think about how mad she might be about not talking to her all summer and set her attention back on Robert. "Can you give me a new copy of it?"

"Sure. You might lose however far you got, though. I kind of did a major overhaul of some of it."

"It's fine," Alice said. "I don't have it on my phone anymore."

Lance stopped beside her and leaned in like he had been part of the conversation all along. Across from her, Adam dropped his stuff and took a seat on the couch. "You were offline all summer," Lance noted. "Any chance your dear old dad got hold of that phone of yours?"

Alice nodded.

"Hand it over," he told her. "And your computer."

"Why?" Robert asked, watching dumbly as Alice handed her devices over without any hesitation. "Why were you offline all summer? Sarah posted a photo of you guys at some party and started talking about cameras."

Lance shoved Alice's phone at Robert. "You have your computer, right? Scan this for me."

"You can't just tell me to do shit outside of..." His words died off as Lance gave him a stern look and he relented, taking it and pulling a cable out of his bag along with his computer. Lance put his bags on the table and sat between the two of them, opening up Alice's laptop. Robert's face soon soured at whatever he was finding on there, but Lance's remained unreadable as he went through the computer.

"Grounded?" Adam jumped in as they went silent.

Alice nodded. "My grades weren't great, so Dad thought I should study more," she said. "No phone, no internet."

"Go anywhere?" he asked.

Alice knew what he was really asking. "Nope," she said. "I couldn't get away."

"At all? You always seem to find a way when you're here."

Alice looked at him, finding herself more tired than frustrated. "At all," she told him.

Adam didn't look happy about it, but he stopped pressing. He looked up and behind her, nodding at someone coming close. "Look who's back," he said. "Did you get the keys?"

Alice looked back to see Adrianna smiling broadly with several keys in her hands. "Hey Alice," she said, giving her a one armed hug as she plopped herself down on the sofa arm next to her. She held out a key triumphantly to her brother with the other hand. "And of course I did. Just have to know how to ask."

"It's nice to have you terrifying again," Adam said, smiling.

"Maybe you should try being *nice* once in a while." Adrianna smiled back and passed a key to Robert and Alice as well, each of them with a small slip of paper with their names and room numbers attached. Alice glanced back to find that they hadn't quite opened yet, though she thought better than to ask just how Adrianna managed to get them. She gladly took her key and room assignment, glad that she was still rooming with Adrianna this year.

Alice saw Heather arrive and offered her a wave. So far everything had been going pretty well, with Robert not pressing or even seeming to believe anything that Sarah had told him. It was as much as Alice could have hoped for, though Heather ignored her and went immediately to Adam.

"Hey. Long time no see."

Alice shifted in her seat as Heather took a seat next to Adam. She opened her mouth to say something, but Heather wouldn't even look at her. As conversation moved to recapping their vacations, Heather skipping any details about her own and pressing Adam for details on his, and Alice quietly gathered her bags. So Heather was still mad at her. Best to let her enjoy herself while Alice went elsewhere.

Alice excused herself and went upstairs to see the new dorm room. Room 301 in this building was different than the last one, but also very similar. There were still the wardrobes and dressers, still a desk to each side and a bed for each, but these beds were much taller to allow for more storage underneath them. More places for Alice to hide things.

Alice reached her hand up and it disappeared off of her wrist into the ceiling. There was still space up here, which was all she needed. She could continue to hide what she needed until she was done with Wonderland. If she could do anything with Wonderland again.

Taking a deep breath, she dropped her bag next to her bed and sat on it. High school. She wasn't sure she really wanted this, but she was here anyway. She pinched the inside of her wrist hard and nothing around her so much as flickered. Except for something in the mirror, though she was quick to cut that off.

"Alice?" She looked up to see Adrianna standing in the door with her bag, smiling as she made her way in. "You kind of disappeared down there."

Alice shrugged. "I don't think Heather really wanted me there," she said.

"Yeah," Adrianna said. She took a seat across from her on her bed. "She's still a little mad about the whole thing last year."

"I *had* to ditch her," Alice said. "I had to go to Wonderland."

Adrianna's face wrinkled, but eventually she nodded. "I guess that too. I think it was more the fight you guys had."

"We had a fight?"

"At the movie night," Adrianna told her. She got up and

went to Alice, looking her carefully over. A crease formed between her eyebrows and she reached for Alice's forehead, through hesitated and brought her hand back before she even brushed against her bangs. "You told her to stay out of your business and you didn't want anyone's help."

Alice stared at her, brows furrowed. "I told her I was..."

But she wouldn't have anymore. The way Alice remembered the night, she said she was dying and vanished in the middle of the room. But the Bandersnatch would have made sure that never happened anymore. Everything would have smoothed over into something much more normal and fighting with Heather would have made more sense.

"I guess I did."

"But you didn't, did you?"

Alice let out a sigh. "It doesn't really matter anymore, right?" she asked.

"It matters to you."

"It doesn't," Alice said, careful to look at her as she did. Hoping that Adrianna believed it. Out of the corner of her eye, she could see something that disappeared as soon as she looked.

"You need to stop doing that, Alice," Adrianna said gently. "I'm not going to—"

A knock at the door interrupted them. Adrianna looked upset about it, but Alice was already on her feet and at the door. Lance was on the other side with her phone and computer in hand. "You forgot these," he said, letting himself in.

"Thanks," Alice said, leaving the door open as Lance made himself comfortable at her desk and continued working through her computer. He handed her phone to her and Alice looked at it for only a moment before she put it in her pocket. She looked to Adrianna to see if she knew what he was doing, but she also looked confused and suspicious about his appearance. "What's up?"

"Grounded all summer?" he asked, keeping his voice low.

Alice glanced at the door and moved closer to him. She didn't want her voice to carry out into the hall.

"And you didn't bother going over at all? Or were you just telling Adam that?"

"I couldn't."

"Why not?"

Alice stayed quiet despite the eyes on her, her mind trying to work on something. She should have known this was coming, but she didn't have an answer. Adrianna was looking at her, though Lance continued working on her computer and frowning. His typing slowed for only a moment before he picked it up again and continued asking uncomfortable questions.

"And Ms. Miller didn't finally snap and break you out?"

Alice shook her head. "She got fired."

He didn't like that answer either. "Have you eaten?"

That made Adrianna look concerned, but Alice noticed something else. Something perfectly distracting. Out of the corner of her eye, she could see someone standing in the corner of the room. "We're being watched," Alice said, staring at the corner and waiting.

As soon as Adrianna looked up and Lance joined her. Arthur watching out of the corner of Alice's eye vanished, but Alice didn't stop looking, waiting for him to return. "He's gone," Alice said after a long moment, and let out a breath.

"Has Arthur been following you all summer too?"

Alice shook her head. "Just saw him earlier today."

"And?"

Alice shrugged. "He's not happy."

"Your phone is fine, by the way," Lance said, waving her over. He started clicking through her desktop, showing her where some of the programs were now located and where recovered files were stored. "Rob got the spyware off pretty easy. And no one's gotten into the folder on here, but I've changed the password and location to get to it. I just need you to type in something new here."

Alice leaned over and typed in something she could remember. "Thanks," she said. "Anything I can do for you?"

Lance got up and turned to face her, frowning. "Yeah," he said, meeting her eyes. There was pity there mixed with the anger that made Alice want to balk, but she stayed where she was. Lance hesitated and seemed to soften, deciding whatever he was going to say wasn't worth it. "Call your sister. And don't go back there again." He looked at her for just a little longer before he got up and walked out of the room.

Alice closed the door behind him. "What was that about?" she asked no one in particular.

"He's been worried," Adrianna told her. "Rayne's been worried too. And Sarah said... Are there really cameras in your house?"

Alice felt like leaving. She could leave now. There was no one watching her every move, no one to keep tabs on her. While she was here, she had that freedom. And she should call Lori and tell her she was okay. Lance was right, she needed to get in touch with her.

Adrianna leaned forward, shaking her head and letting out a small cough. Whatever she was going to say was gone with the smile appearing on her face. "Never mind," she said. "I'll catch you up on what you missed over the summer? Apparently Peter disappeared for a week again and Kevin almost got another brother."

Alice relaxed and sat back down on the bed. Part of her knew she needed to learn and to figure out how to fit in again. And that meant making sure she knew what was going on with her friends. She let Adrianna tell her everything and listened as if she were taking notes. She did her best not to look at the mirror, or at the purple eyes watching her from the other side.

CHAPTER 6

School Days

A WEEK IN and Adrianna could barely remember what summer was like. High school was synonymous with homework as far as she was concerned. She wasn't sure how she would make choir fit in with it all this year. Her bag was heavier with larger text books, her schedule fuller with more classes every day. At the end of the night she was drowning in papers and assignments. Her shoulders hurt from carrying it all around. It would have been easier if her locker wasn't on the opposite side of the school.

She envied Alice, whose bag was perpetually empty except for a novel and her computer, pulling her books as she needed from their place in her locker.

Adrianna wondered idly if she had to go to Wonderland and eat one of their treacles to be able to do that too. She knew Alice had a lot of magic books hidden away somewhere in their dorm room. Maybe one of them had a spell in it to at least make her bag a little lighter. As it was, she worried it would burst at the seams. If her locker weren't so far across the school she might use it more, but the one she had been assigned was in the opposite corner from most of her classes. There was no way she could get over there and back in time, so she was stuck carrying everything with her all day.

At least she wasn't bored. Her teachers had all started right away with the subjects without even trying to learn their names first, throwing assignments at them from the very first day. Somehow the days dragged on and flew by, each class going on forever as she tried to absorb all the new information and then over too soon once they had a chance to do any work.

At least math class was the last one for today, and she didn't mind the person sitting next to her. Adam put his head down, ignoring the teacher telling them about how important algebra was to understanding everything from other math equations to how spicy food might be. Adrianna doubted the claims, but Adam was very sure none of this was worthwhile.

"You know when we'll use this?" he asked. "Literally never. I'm too old for this shit."

The corner of Adrianna's lips quirked up as she took notes. "You could have been done with this a year ago if you weren't gone so long," she told him lightly.

He shot a glare up at her and she smiled back. He looked tired as he lowered his forehead back to the table.

"Are you okay?"

"Lance slept over," he said. "Again. Every night this week."

"Why?"

Adam glanced up at the front of the room, but the teacher had his back turned and was writing something on the board as he continued the lecture. "He's trying to avoid his new room-mate. He's got Arthur now. Asshole's going to school here."

There were a lot of things in that statement that Adrianna wanted to unpack, but she didn't have time for any of them as the teacher turned to scan the room for someone to answer him. An equation was written on the board and his eyes fell on the two of them. Adrianna started to try and work out what the answer was, but she wasn't where he was looking. "Adam, what is X?"

Adam dutifully lifted his head from the table as eyes went back to him. He peered at the board for a moment, his lips pursing for only a moment before he had the answer. "34 plus A squared."

"Excellent," the teacher said, looking satisfied as Adam put his head back down. Adam's lack of attention, Adrianna knew, was because of boredom more than not getting the material. He could have moved up in years if he wanted to. He didn't for reasons that Adrianna didn't much care for.

When class had settled away from them once more, Adrianna asked, "Why don't you like him?"

"Seven," he said, not looking up.

Adrianna sat up a little straighter and glanced behind her. Out of the corner of her eye, she caught the image of a boy in a uniform standing at the back of the room, grinning as his eyes stared into the back of her head. He raised a hand to wave at her, the other arm ending before his wrist.

Her heart leapt up in her chest at the realization he was here too, but she kept herself from jumping and making a scene in class. She looked back again, and he was gone.

"He's following you."

Adrianna couldn't object to that. Out of the corner of her eye all week, she had been seeing something. She'd glimpsed blonde hair, the sound of his voice, or just had that feeling that someone was staring at her. Someone that no one else seemed to be able to see. She thought she was going crazy until Alice confirmed that he was, in fact, actually there. She'd apologized like it was her fault, but Adrianna hadn't thought to ask why.

"I need to talk to him," she said.

"Don't. He won't stop."

"How do you know?"

"Because he's an asshole."

Sometimes there was no getting anything out of Adam.

Still, he was helpful to have next to her during class. He didn't need to pay attention to do well, mostly because he didn't really understand the methods that they used and had concocted his own. If she was ever lost with how she was supposed to do it, he could provide an alternative method and, between the two, she could figure out answers to just about anything. She could only hope her teachers wouldn't be mad about not using their methods on the finals.

Not that she would need a lot of help this year. Everything came to her much more smoothly than it ever had last year or the entire time she had been at Lucena Academy. Despite the volume of work, she understood all of her lessons now. Things that had been so hard before were easy and made perfect sense. It was strange how much being in a coma for half a semester had changed things. It was like a veil had lifted after she woke up and she was seeing the world with new eyes.

You're just noticing now. Nice to have you back.

The words echoed in her head and she still didn't know what Lance meant by them. She had been much more curious about what he was talking to Rob about — a secret he was still keeping — but now she wanted to know what he was talking about. Even some things Adam had said made her think there was more going on, that they knew something she didn't.

When class ended, she and Adam headed back to their rooms to drop off bags full of books before meeting everyone at the cafeteria for dinner. They had homework for the weekend, so much that she was sure she might drown in it all. But for tonight, it was over and she was done. She relaxed and rolled her shoulders as she waited outside of Adam's dorm for him to do the same.

"Just ask," Adam told her, swapping his backpack for a wallet and phone before they made their way down the stairs and to the cafeteria.

"Ask what?"

"You want to ask something right?"

"Lance said I was different," Adrianna said. "Not different, but that I was back."

"Because you are," he said. "I don't know if I like it yet."

"But what does that..."

Adrianna decided quickly that it wasn't worth asking. Adam wasn't in the mood to give answers, his face souring as they entered the cafeteria. A group of familiar faces crowded around a table in the middle of a cafeteria bustling with students looking to grab something quickly before whatever clubs they had after school. Sarah waved to let them know where they were and Adrianna waved back.

But that wasn't where Adam's eyes were. He was watching another blonde in the line for food, waiting her turn. And he wasn't happy about it.

"Because I almost saved it and she stopped me," Adam

said before Adrianna could ask. "And she hasn't even gone to try since."

She watched Alice get her food and go to join everyone else, only to come to a stop. At the table, Heather took a seat and launched into something, her hands moving wildly through the air as she went on about whatever was troubling her. Alice stood for only a moment before she took a step back, shrinking into her shoulders and turning away.

Adrianna watched Alice wander off and disappear in the crowd, a lump forming in the back of her throat. Now that she thought of it, Alice hadn't been there much during dinner or lunch lately. Even when they were studying, she had been absent.

They got their dinner and Adrianna kept scanning the crowd, looking for where Alice had gone. Next to her, Adam knocked his shoulder into her back lightly. "Try the theatre," he suggested, not even looking at her as he took his tray and went to join everyone else at the table.

She hesitated, not sure where she should go. The table had seen her already and Alice hadn't. She should probably go join her friends. But Alice had just been spending too much time alone and away from them lately. There was something wrong and ignoring that would eat her up inside. For all she said she was fine, she had a feeling Alice probably wasn't and she needed the company more.

Whipping out her phone, she turned to the door and sent a quick message to apologize. She would see them tomorrow and she was going to see where Alice was. She didn't wait to see if she got a response before she headed out the door and made her way to the theatre with her dinner.

Chapter 7

Unfortunate Truths

ALICE WAS EASY to find. At the top of the steps of the theatre were large, picturesque windows with a ledge so deep it was impossible that they weren't designed for someone to sit in them. Alice curled up inside one of them and leaned against a faint reflection of herself, a tray of food in front of her and almost completely untouched as her eyes stayed down in her book. She looked calm now, almost meditative, but there was something strange about the sight.

Something looked wrong, but she couldn't put her finger on what. Probably that she was here at all, that she had fled their friends for solitude. That she had ultimately decided that she didn't want to talk to them and instead would rather escape to a book. That she wasn't eating dinner. Lance had asked about her eating before and now, Adrianna thought she looked thinner than she had last year.

"Hey," Adrianna said, leaning against the side of the window. "Can I join you?"

"Oh!" Alice jumped, surprised at the company. She uncurled her legs from under her, letting them dangle over the edge of the window until they brushed the floor. "Sure," she said. She put the book back in her bag and moved her tray, giving Adrianna more than enough space to sit.

Adrianna put her tray next to Alice's, using the space between them like a table as they sat in opposite corners of the window. Taking a carrot off her plate, she started to eat as she looked around. The window overlooked a strange little garden that Adrianna had never noticed before, one on the roof. There was a table out there and a couple chairs that looked more recently used than the rest of the overgrown garden.

"Why aren't you in the cafeteria with everyone else?" Alice asked.

Adrianna studied her for a moment. It seemed like an innocent enough question, and Alice didn't appear to be trying to get rid of her. "You weren't there," she said. "You're spending a lot of time alone. Are you okay?"

"I'm fine," Alice told her. Around her things looked more... normal. It all just felt much more normal.

"How's Rayne?"

Alice blinked at her slowly, blue eyes puzzled for only

a moment before she figured it out. "Lori's good," she said. "She's been sending me a lot of articles."

"Articles?"

Alice nodded, looking down at her plate but taking nothing. "Every couple days she sends me another letter of LGBTQ... QI... Those letters. I think she might be worried that our father is going to convince me she's evil."

"How many letters are there?" Adrianna had only ever heard the first four before. She didn't know there were more.

Alice shrugged. "A lot. She just sent B this morning. I don't think she knows how much homework I have."

"*There's so much*," Adrianna agreed. "I don't know how I'm going to do it all."

"You'll be okay," Alice insisted. "Kevin and Heather know what they're doing. Adam too. They'll help."

A shimmer of something else flashed across the corner of her vision, but it was gone as soon as she looked. The window was just what it had been a moment ago, showing only the strange garden. She leaned in closer so that her reflection vanished and she couldn't make out anything strange out there.

"Did you see that?"

"See what?" Alice asked, looking outside.

"Nothing, I guess," Adrianna said. Maybe it was Arthur. "Arthur is following me around."

"You?"

Adrianna nodded and took a small bite of her chicken. "He keeps showing up in my classes. Like, standing in the back of them. I just see him out of the corner of my eye and then he disappears when I turn to look. That's what he did to you, right?"

"Yeah," Alice said. "I'm sorry. He's mad at me about bringing him here. I knew he wanted to get back at me, though. I don't know why he's following you around like that. Does he actually go here now? Or is he like Cat was?"

"I think so?" Adrianna said. "He's rooming with Lance."

"Has he said anything to you?" Alice asked, her eyes wide again as she looked around before she imploringly back at her. Alice's voice was low and quiet as she spoke. "I think he's from somewhere else. Not Neverland or Wonderland, but somewhere else. Maybe if I can send him back, he'll leave you alone."

Behind her, the glass seemed to warp. This time, it wasn't just a flash but something showing up in the reflection. It was a garden very unlike the one behind them, one overgrown with daisies and daffodils that all appeared to have something to say. They crowded around another table with many regal chairs made of something so white they seemed to glow.

Alice leaned back against the frame of the window and stared down at her food, the images around her starting to fade away. If Adrianna wasn't watching it, she might think she was imagining it, but she had seen Alice disappear into Wonderland enough times to know it.

"No," Alice continued. "Sorry, he's probably not talking to you at all, is he? He's just watching and not saying anything, right?"

Adrianna wasn't sure if she should mention what was happening behind her. Alice, she knew, wasn't trying to do that. It looked like an accident, especially how the scene changed and melted from that table into another, one made of stone in a place that seemed to have no source of light though Adrianna could see it fine anyway. It was like she was just thinking about Wonderland a lot. Like she missed it.

Maybe if she wasn't thinking about it anymore that would stop. She needed to try something that wasn't about Wonderland to see if that would help.

"Alice?" she asked finally. "What happened with you and Heather?"

"We had a fight," Alice said, a little too quickly and without any hint of sadness. "She doesn't want to talk to me anymore."

"Sarah said you disappeared after that fight," Adrianna pressed. "You weren't back until graduation. Did something else happen that night?"

Alice didn't say anything for a very long time. She kept watching Adrianna like she was thinking very carefully about her words. Adrianna tried to keep her attention on Alice and how small she seemed now. How she looked like she might disappear from in front of her at any moment. Given who she was talking to, that was definitely something that could happen.

She tried not to look at the window and the strange other world in the reflection. Everything about Alice was inevitably about Wonderland.

The silence stretched on unbearably and Adrianna had to break it or they would fall into it forever. Wonderland or not, she should at least ask. It was bothering Alice and maybe talking about it would help. "You've been different since the year started. What happened?"

Alice stayed quiet, bringing her knees up in front of her, carefully curling her legs around her so that her skirt would not fall out of place. She held them loosely in her arms like protection. She didn't look tense or worried otherwise, but she so rarely ever did.

"That fight with Heather," she said slowly, testing. Her eyes went up to Adrianna, but she wasn't looking at her. She was looking at something far beyond anything in this theater. "I don't... I don't know what everyone thinks happened that night. I kind of yelled at her and just disappeared in front of everyone. I mean, I still yelled at Heather. But I told her... something else."

"What did you tell her?"

The silence returned, but Adrianna didn't know that she should push it again. She put down her fork, putting her attention on Alice as she pulled herself in tighter and her gaze moved down to her knees. After seconds that felt like hours, Alice was ready to continue.

"I wasn't supposed to come back," Alice said, her voice barely above a whisper that seemed to echo in the large, empty space. She wouldn't look at Adrianna when she spoke and she could see her eyes growing more and more watery with every word. "It wasn't supposed to matter because the Bandersnatch was supposed to win."

A lot had just happened in only a few words and Adrianna was very careful not to move, certain that Alice would bolt at the slightest chance. She was sure the shock on her own face was clear and she could do nothing to hide it. Alice didn't think she was going to make it. After all her insistence that the Bandersnatch was dealt with, she had expected to go into the lair and to disappear forever. She was planning to...

And if she had, Adrianna would have never known. Her memory of Alice would have been gone and she would have lived on without her. That almost hurt more.

"What happened?" she asked. She couldn't help herself. She didn't know if she wanted the answer or an explanation or an apology. Right now, she just wanted Alice to keep talking and hoped an idea would appear.

"Adam tried to make a deal with him." Alice's eyes found a spot on the floor and watched it carefully. "I wasn't saving Wonderland, so he tried to make a deal. I tried to offer myself first, but he wouldn't let me."

"Adam?" Adrianna asked. She didn't press this time, letting the silence linger in the air. This wasn't the direction she was hoping for.

"I don't know what to do anymore," Alice admitted. She was trembling and her knuckles were going white against her legs as she pulled them in closer. "I wasn't supposed to still be here. I tried to stay in Wonderland for as long as I could, but the Bandersnatch only covered me until the end of the semester. I can't put the hearts back without getting dizzy anymore, so I wasn't any use there. Heather and Adam both hate me here. Rob doesn't want to talk to me or he'll make Heather mad. I don't know what I'm supposed to do anymore." She buried her face in her knees, her voice growing quieter. "It would have been easier if he had just taken me."

Words passed across her mind, but none of them would linger long enough for her to speak any of them. Assurances that no one hated her dissipated as soon as she said that last thing. It would have been easier if she had been taken. If she had disappeared and no one ever remembered her. If she were gone.

Behind them, the garden was gone, replaced with a wall of red. The texture shifted and moved in a regular rhythm that she could almost hear.

Adrianna didn't know what to do or what to say. Alice was so still, so small. She always seemed so confident before, like she knew exactly what she was doing. Scared and overwhelmed at times, but never like this. How long had she been like this? She lived with Alice. She saw her every day. She should have known.

Gently, she reached over to put a hand on Alice's shoulder. Alice jumped as soon as she made contact, her head snapping up and her eyes wide as she stared back at her. She looked much too fragile, like she could crumble at any moment. "I'm happy you're still here," Adrianna said, trying to smile. "We can figure something out."

Dully, Alice nodded. "Yeah." Alice glanced behind her, spotting the red wall behind her and the image cut itself off. "Sorry," she said, shifting back into the window frame.

Adrianna could feel Alice studying her, though she wouldn't quite look at her. She didn't know where else to go, what else to say about it, but she did have an idea. "When's the last time you went to Wonderland?" she asked.

Alice let out a breath and let go of her legs. "Not since June. But there's no point if I can't put the hearts back."

"Why not?" she asked.

"I don't know," she said. "Peter said it might have something to do with those danishes. Claudia might have done something."

"Claudia?"

Alice's eyes narrowed on her. She relaxed, her feet sliding off the edge of the windowsill as she peered at Adrianna. "Your stepmother. Claudia."

"Oh," Adrianna said. "She's gone now."

"Gone? What do you mean gone?"

Adrianna shrugged. "She's gone."

The look on Alice's face looked so much like Evan's when she told him the same thing. They both knew something, despite never talking to one another. And neither was forthcoming with that information. Right now, Adrianna didn't want to press. Alice was coming back to her normal self already.

"You're okay with me going back to Wonderland?" Alice asked instead.

Adrianna nodded. "Try again to put the hearts back," she said. "And if you can't, maybe you can teach me. You don't have to do it alone anymore. I can help." And while Alice was in Wonderland, Adrianna could figure out how to repair the hurt feelings between her and Heather.

Alice smiled and nodded. "Thanks," she said, relaxing in the windowsill. Adrianna could see the old Alice come back, and she felt the tension in her stomach finally let go. Maybe a weekend in Wonderland would be good for her. And when she got back, Adrianna would know how she could actually help.

CHAPTER 8

Weekend Retreat

AS SOON AS she was across, Alice realized how much she missed Wonderland. Or maybe it was just knowing that she wouldn't have to be in any awkward situations for a weekend, no having to speak carefully when Heather was around, no having to quietly excuse herself when it was clear she wasn't wanted. Adrianna said she would help try to figure out something, but Alice wasn't holding out much hope that she could change Heather's mind.

It was fine. Not everyone was going to like her. No need to cause more problems by being there and making things awkward. They could have a nice weekend on their own.

Alice didn't know why she asked Adrianna how she felt about her going to Wonderland. Adrianna had never had much of an opinion about her going, only that she wanted to know that Alice had gone at all. Maybe she just needed someone else to tell her no. That she shouldn't come here. That she didn't have to face the disappointment any longer.

Of course, Adrianna hadn't. And now, here she was.

"She has seen fit to return," Cat said, slinking around her shoulders soon after she arrived. She had only made it a couple steps, but Alice had felt him watching her with a mix of disdain and impatience for the whole summer. "Have you decided to come to a madness that realizes who you are?"

"Hello Cat," Alice said, not bothering to try and detach herself as she kept walking. "Has much changed since I was here last?"

"So much business," Cat chided her. "But I think we know that you are not here for that. You have come to escape. I know you have not decided that you care so much about our home that you will fix it."

"Adrianna thinks I can put the hearts back now," she said.

"The pretty one is hopeful that you became useful."

Alice said nothing and let him continue, moving through Wonderland at a casual pace. With every step, he followed along beside her and chattered about whatever he wanted. Alice thought it best to at least try to find out what was going on. "What have I missed?" Alice asked. "Has the Queen moved?"

"The Queen of Hearts has taken in a guest and remained in her castle," he said. "She has not left since you left us."

Alice frowned. "Who did she get?" she asked. It can't

have been anyone too important. Otherwise, Cat would have harassed her much more, not that she could do anything to help in her current state. They both were very aware of that.

"Only a guest," Cat assured her. "A guest who has seemed to place some very interesting ideas in her head."

"Have you been in the castle?"

"Few enter the castle any longer," he said. "They leave, but we have not permitted them back. Hatter is getting quite annoyed that we cannot get inside anymore. He continues to insist that we listen to you about that monster in the woods. You bring us another monster that we cannot use. That dragon was bad enough, Alice dear. You did not have to bring another. We do not want them."

"You're stuck with him now," she said. "Just leave him alone and you'll be fine."

"Perhaps you should have not sent something that the Queen wanted to talk to so badly."

Alice kept walking until she found herself walking closer to where Tiger Lily was. She wanted an actual update, one that wasn't enshrouded in riddles that she couldn't quite make out. She knew Cat could speak plainly, but he was very adamant about not doing so if he could help it. And he was very good at that.

The door was already parted when Alice arrived at the front of her tent and she let herself in. Tiger Lily was not there, but there was a small grey rabbit currently rummaging through her things with a distinct gap in his chest partially hidden by his waistcoat. Alice didn't like that much at all.

"Hey!" she said, getting his attention. The rabbit didn't stop his search, continuing to go through her things as if Alice wasn't there.

"I believe you are supposed to stop him," Cat told her helpfully. "Or are you unable to do even that?"

Alice groaned and went in, going closer to the rabbit and grabbing him by the shoulder. She pulled him back gently, but it didn't deter him. "Hey," she said, unsure of just what she was supposed to do. Without his heart, the rabbit might not pay much attention to her. Only some of the heartless people of Wonderland maintained any autonomy after their hearts were removed. "I don't think it's very polite to be going through another person's things if they aren't here. You should wait and ask first, at the very least."

Cat chuckled but didn't help, instead coming closer to taunt her. "This is not how you deal with a thief so brazen," Cat said, taking a swipe at the rabbit. "But you have no idea how to be a predator. You are more mouse than cat, Alice dear. Allow me to show how you deal with prey."

Alice saw the grin on his face, the teeth that appeared, and she latched onto him before he could vanish. No, she wasn't going to let him spill blood in a house that was not his own.

Or at all, if she could help it. This was Wonderland where people were civilized. There was a proper order of things, and this was...

This was...

Her grip relaxed as she felt a headache creeping into the back of her mind. Oh, that wasn't right at all. She felt very strange and like she might want to take a very long nap immediately. This was not the time and she pushed that feeling back.

"Another," a voice growled at the door. Tiger Lily moved quickly and seized the rabbit by the scuff of the collar, hauling him out of the tent and away from there. Alice continued to watch nothing as Cat squirmed out of her arms and disappeared. "Interesting," he muttered, and she could feel his violet eyes watching her.

Alice stood alone for a long moment, trying to keep her balance and understand what was going on in her head. When none of it made any sense, she shook it and let out a deep breath, looking around to find Tiger Lily back and watching her as well. "Hi," she said. "The door was open. I saw him in here and..."

"Hello, Alice of Wonderland," Tiger Lily said. "Sit. Have some tea. I will make it. It has been a while. We have much to discuss."

"Like the rabbit that tried to rob you?" Alice asked.

"They look for the books you have left with me," she said,

already pouring a pair of tea cups. Alice took a seat on the floor, ignoring the table. "They have not found them. Not yet. I expect to return them to you."

Alice nodded. "I didn't get taken," she said. "I should have gotten them from you the last time."

"Have you found someone in your world who may learn the secrets of the books?"

In the month she had spent in Wonderland after her victory against the Bandersnatch, the topic had come up frequently. It wasn't just that Alice couldn't put the hearts back. She couldn't cast any of the spells she had learned from the books at all. Tiger Lily wasn't the only one upset that they had lost a valuable asset in their fight, but she was the only one who thought it would be best for Alice to try and find someone outside of Wonderland to help. Especially since she had been unable to find anyone in Wonderland who could pay attention long enough to learn anything before erupting into complaints and criticisms.

"I don't know," Alice said. "Adrianna couldn't read them before but she's been different since she woke up. If not her, maybe Lance would do it. Are there a lot more hearts to return?"

"It has been a long time since you've been to Wonderland," Tiger Lily said, as if that were answer enough.

Alice nodded. "Sorry," she said. She was sure she didn't

have to explain to Tiger Lily, and she didn't want to say it again. She was useless here. She couldn't return the hearts, so she had seen no point in even trying. Still, she didn't appear to press it, instead pushing a cup into Alice's hands and looking her over. "You are no happier than before," she noted. "You are still upset about your survival."

"Of course I'm happy I survived," Alice snapped back at her. "I just wish I could actually do something."

"Retrieve your books and find a cure for yourself," Tiger Lily suggested. "You may also wish to attend the tea party. They have been insufferable and you have been missing for a very long time."

Alice let out a sigh and nodded, drinking her tea. Tiger Lily also managed to push a few tarts from the fridge onto her and waited until she had finished eating them before she led her into the forest to the tea party.

Despite the quiet settling over Wonderland, the forest didn't fully shut up. There was a chattering around them as they went, and Alice could feel the eyes of birds and flowers watching their every step, likely talking among themselves about how rude they were for not saying hello. A cat with a puzzled expression and no hole in her chest ushered her bickering kittens along to a small hut deep in the woods.

The animals weren't all that caught her attention. A large

shape moved in the distance, only just visible through the trees. The Queen of Heart's castle was on the horizon, lingering just a little too close to the barrier.

That wasn't where the castle was meant to be. It certainly wasn't where she had left it. Wonderland was strange, but the castle felt like it was moving with intent. If it was the Queen of Heart's intent, then nothing good would come of allowing it to keep wandering.

"It keeps getting closer to Neverland," Tiger Lily noted as she led the way to the long table adorned with tea that would never be drunk and took a seat. Alice sat next to her, gazing around at the familiar faces at the table. They had a turtle serving them very slowly, wandering aimlessly back and forth around the table with a teapot, occasionally pouring nothing at all into the cups. At the end was the grey rabbit in a waistcoat tethered to a chair, no longer rummaging through Tiger Lily's belongings but looking like he was ready to run and do it again as soon as he was released.

"A watched pot does not boil any more than a watched castle moves," the Dormouse noted between yawns from inside his sugar bowl. "I am not asleep. Only resting my eyes. I can hear you all. Very rude to speak as if I'm not here."

"Very rude to rest your eyes at a party!" The Mad Hatter countered.

"Is there anything I can do?" Alice asked. They didn't

seem to have missed her, but she knew she would likely be put to work soon enough. "I have all weekend."

"The ends are so sad," The Mad Hatter noted. "Much worse than the beginnings. Beginnings are much more full of hope. Endings are much too final."

"There's always a sequel," the Dormouse told him.

"And spinoffs," Alice added. "And Sarah says fan fiction is also really good if you want more."

"Why, I don't want to read about fans!" Hatter said. "Terribly dull conversations, never want to take any action unless you force them. And even when they do, it is only as much as they must!"

"The hearts remain trapped in the castle," Cat purred at her, curling up in front of her. "None have entered and left since you. Perhaps you could do something useful and—"

"Not her," came a voice Alice hadn't heard in a very long time. She looked around the table, finding that the Caterpillar was sitting nowhere in sight. She looked under the table and saw the smoke rings flowing up from his very small perch. He regarded her shoe very carefully as Alice looked under, and others joined her in the small conference. "Make that Cat do it."

"Why not me?"

"The Queen is only a Queen because she says she is," the Caterpillar said.

"Yes, that is how Queens occur," Tiger Lily said. She sounded irritated, like she had endured this conversation far too many times already and she wanted no more part of it.

"She remains the Queen because she believes it."

"What is your point, bug?"

He snapped around to glare at Tiger Lily, though she did not back down. She was no more used to dealing with Wonderland than she had ever been, but Alice did quite enjoy watching Wonderland get under her skin. "I have only met one other girl so rude," he said. "A shame you have both met. It seems that you will combine soon."

Tiger Lily groaned and sat back on the ground, rolling her eyes. "It pains me to agree," Tiger Lily relented. "You would do best not to go. Cat has not been nearly so useful. He has much more to prove to ensure his usefulness."

"You assume a cat is meant to be useful," Cat snarled. "A cat is meant only for their own means and not for any other meaning but the meaning that they mean."

"Why not me?" Alice asked. "If you please. I can get in and out pretty easily. I know my way around." She didn't *like* being in there, by any means, but she was comfortable enough with the idea and knew how to get where she needed to if she had to. She could find the hearts.

"There is another Queen," he said. The clouds around

him parted and the Caterpillar stared hard at her, trying to impart how serious he was. He looked very unlike Wonderland in that moment, old and like he was something else entirely. "One who is far older, far different, and who does not belong here. You and I, we must stay far away from her. Many of us must. You stay on your side of the mirror. Stay far away and let her try to do her bidding without the heart of Wonderland."

Alice watched him for a long moment, but he took another drag on his hookah and calmed down soon enough. Tiger Lily did not look impressed, instead waiting for him to be done and looking behind her like she was looking for anywhere else she could be.

"I believe I will become a butterfly soon," he said. "I wish to fly away from here. Before…"

"But what does bring you back, Alice?" came a voice above the table. Alice sat back up in her chair, finding the Mad Hatter leaning across the table to stare a little too closely into her face. "Perhaps your gift of filling unfortunate holes has returned?"

His smile was too hopeful and she didn't want to disappoint. "Maybe," she said, though she very sure the answer was no. "I don't have a heart right now, though."

"Oh, not to worry," he said, tipping his hat. Front inside, he drew out a small box and presented it to her, wrapped delicately with a bow. "We have been saving this for when you returned. Open it."

Alice already knew what she would find inside. She could feel it pulsing in her hands, could hear it beating softly in her ears. She pulled the ribbon and opened the top, finding the heart inside, one she knew belonged to their thief of a rabbit.

Of course they would have a heart wrapped and ready for her. Of course they would.

"You're too kind." She took it out and let out a deep sigh. The only thing left to do was try and fail. Nothing had changed about her since the last time she was in Wonderland. There was nothing left to do but try again and see if she could push herself enough to do this even once.

Heart cradled in her hand, she closed her eyes to keep herself steady, but already she could feel a wave of dizziness hit her. The overwhelming feeling that the words and motions were mad at her hit in a wave, telling her she was not supposed to be doing this.

She got to her feet and planted them solidly on the ground. Maybe if she forced herself enough, this time it would work. Alice pressed forward, ignoring the unease in her head and her body's urging for her to find something solid to fall onto while it recovered. Her voice was shaky, but she made herself continue, even as she felt her limbs tremble. Her weight was fully against the table when the heart still left her hand and found the chest. She turned her wrist, first the wrong way then the right one, until the heart settled back in place.

Tiger Lily caught her before she hit her head on the table, lowering her back into her seat. "You are still unwell, Alice of Wonderland."

She'd done it. Alice could hardly believe it, but she'd actually done it. She struggled to drag in enough air into her lungs and her fingers were almost numb from how fiercely they were vibrating, but she had actually done it. Maybe she was finally returning to normal after so long. Maybe, if she just kept pushing herself, maybe she could go back to being useful again.

"Why I never!" came the cries of the rabbit, incredulous at his conditions. "I have no recollection of coming to this place! Surely, if I did not bring myself here, then you must have done it!" He squinted at Tiger Lily, then jumped backwards as his memory returned and he realized who she was.

"But," the rabbit said, looking carefully over Tiger Lily, "I do believe it is best not to be hasty. No need to draw out anything unfortunate. I must say, it's terribly uncivilized for such a lovely young woman as—"

"She won't hurt you," Alice said. Her head was pounding and she suddenly felt very light instead of very heavy. "Though I would hardly blame her. You decided that

simply walking into another person's home and helping yourself was appropriate! Even without a lock, a closed
door is still a door and I daresay I don't think you even
knocked!"

"Oh dear," the rabbit said. "I daresay I didn't. I just had a
need to find those damned books. A silly thing for a rabbit to
look for. I never learned to read, you see, and the books might
not even have pictures. What use is a book without pictures?"

"There are quite a few interesting words you might find,"
Alice said. "I am quite a fan of Pumpernickel, myself."

"The woman wanted them," the rabbit told Tiger Lily.
"She said nothing, but somehow I knew she wanted them. It
wasn't for myself, no."

Tiger Lily frowned at the horizon. "Would you like to
take a walk, Alice of Wonderland? I have hidden the books
very far away."

"Already taking her away from us again?" Hatter asked,
looking disappointed. "We have so many more hearts!"

"She isn't well," Tiger Lily insisted. "You cannot make
her continue like this. It's time for her to try to find another
from her own world."

"Wonderland has more than enough problems already
without bringing in more people without manners," Hatter
said. "If Alice can do it, then she very well should! A little
more practice is all—"

"Yeah," Alice said. Her head was already pounding and the arguing was not helping. "A very long walk would be good."

Chapter 9

Filling the Gaps

EMBEDDED INTO THE back of the high school dorms was a small coffee shop called Bean. It had taken a week for them to figure out it was there at all. It was more of a kiosk than anything else, open sporadically during the week and manned by a local shop leasing the space. The drinks were mediocre at best, but it seemed like the best place to grab Heather for fifteen minutes between her other commitments.

Adrianna only got Heather for ten minutes, but it was a very enlightening ten minutes about how Heather was mad but not that mad at Alice. She was much more frustrated with how unreliable Alice was, how Heather had reached out to help her, and she was sick of Alice turning her down at every turn by ghosting her instead of just telling her no. She was done with it and she didn't want to waste her energy on trying to help her any longer.

Heather had to rush off, leaving Adrianna nursing a barely touched tea. At least she knew where to start. She sent Rayne a text, hoping that she could make the first of her ideas happen. The rest would have to rely on Alice talking to Heather without being so worried about bothering her. She could go with her if Alice needed her. It wasn't too late, at least. Not yet.

Rayne wanted to know if Alice was getting her emails, and Adrianna sat at the table messaging back and forth with Rayne, letting her know what was going on here and getting updates about Ryan's wedding. Apparently Rayne had stepped in to help with some planning and was getting very invested.

"Addie?" Adrianna looked up from her phone and smiled at Sarah as she leaned across the table. Her hair was loose around her shoulders today instead of tied up in a messy bun atop her head, and she wore purple and white in subtle layers. She looked pretty and Adrianna tried to remember if she mentioned any plans for today. "You want some company?"

"Sure!" Adrianna said, letting Rayne know she had company before she put the phone down. "Didn't you have a dentist thing this weekend?"

Sarah rolled her eyes and let out an annoyed sound. "Don't

remind me. It's tomorrow. Six more months before I get these braces off."

"Your teeth are going to look amazing."

"I am going to ruin them with coffee immediately." Sarah laughed, looking back to the now closed kiosk. Adrianna hadn't even seen them shut down, but Sarah had already resigned herself to the lack of caffeine. "I swear, they are *never* open when I'm here."

"They don't really have regular hours," Adrianna agreed. "Maybe when they see how many people like it, they'll keep it open."

"They should just move into the dorms," Sarah said. "They'll make plenty and I can develop a habit. Look, I have motives today, Addie. I need to ask you about Wyatt."

Adrianna hadn't been expecting that. "Wyatt?"

"You two were a thing once," Sarah said. She opened her mouth to say more, but she stopped, confusion fluttering across her face. Her eyes narrowed on Adrianna and she closed her mouth, pursing her lips as she studied her. "Do you remember having a thing with Wyatt?"

"Yes?" It had been years ago. Adrianna wasn't sure why it had ended, but at the time she had definitely fallen for him. She'd even dragged Alice along with her and, looking back on it now, that had been a terrible idea. "It was ages ago."

"Okay," Sarah said. "We weren't sure. Everything with that stuff's a little..." She waved her hand between them as an explanation.

Adrianna stared at her for what felt like too long before she finally figured it out. "The Bandersnatch, right?" she asked to be sure, but she was pretty sure that's what that was. Alice had told her about it. Even Evan had told her about it. She didn't know why it was so hard to remember.

"Yeah," Sarah said. "Look, I think he's going to ask me out. And I just wanted to make sure you were cool with it. After last time, I don't want to start anything else."

"It's fine with me," Adrianna told her. She didn't really know why she was asking at all. Adrianna and Wyatt had barely even talked in years. The more surprising thing was that Sarah and Wyatt were talking. "How did you guys meet? I mean, is it just in class or...?"

"Book Club," Sarah blurted out. She caught herself after it was out and offered a grin. She glanced around and leaned in, waving her conspiratorially closer. "Sort of. It's kind of... It's a bunch of us who all got taken meeting up to chat. Some of us have been talking and it might be good for Alice if you think she's interested."

Adrianna considered it, but her mind quickly went elsewhere. Sarah had mentioned it before, but somehow Adrianna hadn't quite put it together. Like Evan, she could remember all the things that the monster in the woods made people forget. Maybe she knew even more.

"I'll ask her," Adrianna said. "Okay, this might be a weird question, but do you remember when Heather and Alice had that fight? Do you know what really happened?"

Sarah pulled a sour face, pulling away to the other side of the table while her eyes stayed on Adrianna. Slowly, she opened her mouth, then closed it again and she thought about it for just a moment longer. "What did Alice tell you?"

The memory of what Alice told her yesterday was still a little too fresh and Adrianna still hadn't processed it yet. "She didn't really say what happened," Adrianna said. "Just that it wasn't the same as what I remembered. So I'm guessing she didn't just tell Heather to back off and leave her alone."

"She said she was dying and then she vanished."

Well. That made the memory of the conversation last night come back a little too sharply. All those feelings she hadn't figured out came rushing back. Alice had said about the same thing, but somehow Adrianna hadn't put it so bluntly yet in her own mind. Maybe she hadn't wanted to. Her chest was tight and the guilt welled up in her. "Oh."

But that could change now. Adrianna knew about it, so she could do something to help her fix it. She was already trying to figure out how to put her life here back together.

This double life was wearing on her so, once this was settled, she would have a life waiting for her when she was finally done with Wonderland. And Adrianna might be able to help her wrap that up as well. She just needed to find a way and it would be okay.

"Hey," Sarah said, reaching over to her. "This is going to sound crazy, but don't push her too much, okay? She's going to have to do some of this for herself. You need to wait for her to come to you."

"She might not," Adrianna pointed out. There was no point in trying to deny what she was thinking. "I mean, she—"

Adrianna stopped, seeing Wyatt walking over. "Maybe we'll do this later?" Adrianna asked, sitting up straighter and watching as he approached.

He stopped behind Sarah and looked between the pair, concerned. "Are you okay?" he asked.

"We're good," Sarah said. "Addie's going to extend the invite to Alice for the Book Club."

Adrianna nodded. "Adam might also—"

"No," they both said. Only Wyatt continued. "Adam is absolutely not invited."

"Why not?"

"Ask him what he did." It was short, but Adrianna didn't think she'd ever heard vitriol in Wyatt's voice before. That

Sarah didn't seem to flinch at it was surprising, but she didn't look apologetic for it either. "You coming?"

"Later," Sarah said as a promise, leaving Adrianna alone at the table and rushing after Wyatt.

Adrianna put her head down on the table. She didn't know how it had gotten so complicated. She'd been here this whole time. She thought Alice was telling her everything, but she had missed so much. The more she talked to everyone else, the bigger the story got. When did all of this happen?

Everything's always been happening Addie.

She should really talk to Lance about all of this. He didn't look surprised at all about anything she told him about what was happening and she needed someone who understood what was going on. Somehow, Lance seemed to know everything. At least, he could talk about all of this with her. Maybe she could run a few things by him to figure out how to make this all work out and make Alice happy again.

It would be nice to see Alice smiling again. She could barely remember the last time there was one on her face and she wasn't sure how many of them were real.

Adrianna raised her head and jumped. She was no longer alone at the table. Across from her, Arthur had stolen what remained of her tea and discarded the lid, drinking directly from the cup with a sour expression. His blonde hair was brushed out of his brown eyes, his sharp jaw crooked as he regarded her drink. "None of you know how to make a decent cup of tea," he complained, though he drank it anyway.

"You've been following me," Adrianna said. It all felt like too much for one hour, but she needed to ask him about this. "I keep seeing you out of the corner of my eye. Why are you watching me?"

"Who wouldn't want to watch such a beauty?" Arthur asked. If he hadn't been following her so profusely, the butterflies in her stomach might have fluttered so hard they would consume her. As it was, Adrianna couldn't help the flush. "It's been far too long since I've laid my eyes on someone so lovely."

"What do you want from me?" Adrianna asked. She knew she shouldn't be flattered and she didn't like what he was doing at all. Attractive or not, he was being very creepy. "I can't do... whatever it is you..."

"Ah, but you can do everything I need," he assured her. Gently, he took her by the hand. "All I need is a night."

Adrianna felt her heart thump heavily in her chest and she pushed herself to her feet. She was flattered and scared all at once, and she didn't like where any of this was going. She knew nothing about him except that he was being mean to Alice. He was also following her around, lingering at the edge of her vision and apparently just watching her whenever he felt like it.

And attractive. He was also very attractive. And he thought she was beautiful.

"I have to go," Adrianna said, gathering her purse and leaving as fast as her feet would carry her. Hopefully, her room would provide solitude where Arthur wouldn't follow her. Alice wouldn't be back yet. She needed a chance to be alone and try to put these thoughts in order.

CHAPTER 10

Passing Knowledge

ALICE EMERGED THROUGH the mirror a little after five in the morning, arms filled with the books that she had hidden away in Wonderland. She left the journals chronicling the last couple years behind. She hadn't written a new one in a while and didn't see herself starting again. That lingering feeling that someone was watching her every move remained and even the thought of a new journal made her anxious.

She set the books on her desk and opened up the computer. It was still too early to be awake, but she didn't feel the slightest bit tired. Her walk through Wonderland and talking to Tiger Lily had been mostly relaxing, despite seeing what had changed. The Queen's withdrawal into the castle was giving Wonderland a chance to heal, but it had also left a lot of its people wandering aimlessly through the land. But no longer were they worried that they were going to be ambushed in an effort to expand the army. Instead, many of the heartless people of Wonderland were taken in by friends and family, scolded for their manners, and put to work. Where they could, they gave retrieved hearts to the families so they could manage it, but Tiger Lily had stopped Alice from returning any to their bodies.

But she *could*. It had been difficult and draining, almost too much for her to handle, but she had done it.

She felt light, accomplished. When the dizziness passed, she couldn't quite get rid of the smile on her face. She could do it again. She could do the one thing that Wonderland really needed her to do. Soon, she could be useful to them again. Soon she could do what she was there for.

The feeling hadn't faded yet as Alice went back to the open tabs on her computer and the emails that Lori had sent. There were more now, more letters of the acronym that needed attention now being given to her out of order. Mixed in amidst them was an email from her mother with an attachment that she ignored. Whatever it was, she was sure she didn't need Alice to respond well before she was awake.

Instead, Alice went back to the B email from Lori. Reading through the article on bisexuality, Alice wondered what the point of any of this really was. Lori was interested in other girls. Wasn't that all she really needed to know? But Lori said she wanted her to understand the whole world and all the different people in it and how they all loved, not just her.

Alice felt strange as she read through it. This one was written as if the writer was talking directly to her and it sucked her in. People who were attracted to other people whether they were a boy or a girl. Alice didn't think that sounded quite right, but she knew that she hadn't felt particularly different about boys or girls. She had the same amount of interested in both, whether she knew whether they were a boy or a girl.

Was she...?

Alice closed the laptop. She could pick up Lori's articles another day. It wasn't even 6 am yet, but she could probably read a couple more chapters of her novel before Adrianna woke up. She let herself plunge back into the fictional worlds, fantastic battles, and interpersonal drama, the article fading from the back of her mind. She started under the covers, lighting the pages with her phone, then moved above them as the sun started to rise and gave her enough light to read by.

She heard Adrianna muttering and looked over, finding her eyes fluttering open. Alice put the slip of paper back into her book to mark her place and sat up, smiling as Adrianna blinked a few times and let out a low grumble.

"Alice?"

"Hi," Alice said.

"Monday?"

"Sunday."

"You're back early," she mumbled. Slowly, she opened her eyes and then narrowed them on Alice. "Did it go okay? Did you get hurt?"

"It was fine," Alice said. "Wonderland isn't changing much since the Queen's decided to lock herself in the castle. They think something's happening, but so long as Tiger Lily keeps an eye on the castle to make sure it doesn't move it might be okay for a while. A watched castle doesn't move, right?"

"That..." Adrianna started, but she stopped and caught herself and pushed herself up in bed. "Wonderland must have been a lot of fun before all of this," she said. "Do you know what you have to do to get it back to normal?"

Alice shook her head. "Let the Queen go to Neverland? I mean, if she's there, then she's not doing things to Wonderland anymore, right?"

"That would make it easy," Adrianna said. "But now that you're back, I think I've figured out a few things to make your life here a bit better. I think you have an email from your mom."

Obediently, Alice went to her computer and went back to the email from her mother. She glanced back, Adrianna looking far too expectant as she opened it. It was still much too early to send her back anything, but clearly Adrianna knew something that she didn't. There was no harm in looking at it now, at least.

Alice,

I miss you so much. I hope you did all right at your father's this summer. I'm working to try and get him to let you come here, but you know how he is. It's been difficult, but I have been able to talk to your sister. She is doing well and says hi, and I've realized just how much I miss you both when you are away. It makes me wish I could homeschool you both just so I don't have to miss so much of your lives. I am not happy about her choices, but she's my daughter and I love her. She is also much more stubborn than you are.

I've found a new job in New York and am adjusting to the city. The Cases have been very kind and helped considerably in getting me resettled. I hope you can come see. I've got enough space here if you and your sister if you ever get the option to come live with me.

Lori tells me that you've been wanting to join a club and your father has said no. I am still your mother and I see no problem with letting you join. I've attached the permission slip. Please have fun and be careful.

Love,
Mom

"Combat Club?" Alice asked, looking at the attachment. A signed permission slip. She had wanted this before, but now...

Adrianna had rolled out of bed by the time Alice had finished reading and was lingering over Alice's shoulder, her eyes flickering between Alice and the stack of books next to her. She covered her mouth and let out a yawn, wiping at her eyes. "So you don't have to keep sneaking out to take lessons from Peter," she said. "You've been basically doing it for a while with him anyway."

"That's Heather's club now, though," Alice said. She didn't want to intrude on a place that Heather felt like was her own. Or interact with her at all while she was still mad. She had more or less given up on the club at this point. Now that she was allowed to go, she wasn't sure she really could without getting Heather's say so first. And she couldn't get that if Heather wouldn't acknowledge she was even there.

"Heather's not mad at *you* exactly," she explained. "She's just mad that you need help and you won't do anything about it. And she also isn't going to believe you if you say you're doing anything, so if you show her you're trying to do something she'll probably at least stop with the silent treatment."

"Will she like me again?"

Adrianna looked gently at her, pity in her eyes. "You need to actually talk to her, Alice," she said. "I can't do that for you." She hooked her arms around Alice's shoulders and gave her a squeeze. "One thing at a time," she said. "You wanted to join anyway. Now you get to."

"Yeah," Alice nodded. Getting Heather to talk to her again. It might just be worth it. And she could finally learn how to not get taken so badly when Wonderland decided to throw punches. Or Tiger Lily did. Peter had helped, but it was only so much. "I hope she's okay with it."

"She will be, " Adrianna assured her, looking back to the desk. "And now that we have that settled, why did you take all the books out?"

"Oh, I brought them back from Wonderland," Alice told her, closing the lid of her laptop and turning back to Adrianna. "I hid them over there last year, but people keep trying to get them. I wondered for a while about how maybe I should find someone over on this side to learn the spells in them so that we had someone else who could return the hearts. No one there could really do it, so I thought maybe there would be someone here."

Adrianna took a seat on Alice's bed and watched her. "Is there a but?" she asked. "You look really happy about something."

Alice shrugged, but she did let a smile pull at her lips. "I can put the hearts back again," she said. "So maybe we don't need to anymore." At the surprise on Adrianna's face, she continued in a flood, "It's not exactly like before. It's a lot harder, but I can actually do it again. I'm going to have to work really hard to do it, but..."

"That's great!"

Alice let the knot in her chest relax. "But now I don't know if we really need to bring anyone else in. No one else really needs to do all of this."

Adrianna was smiling as she leaned forward on the bed. "But I said I was going to help you," she said. "Even if you don't *have to* have someone else who knows it, it would be good to have some help, right? Two people work faster than one. And then you can finish everything Wonderland wants you to do sooner!"

Right. If she put all the hearts back, then Wonderland might be done with her. And if it were done with her, then she might never get to go back again. After all, what would it need her for once she stopped being useful? Once again, she would be out here where she couldn't so much as talk about it for the rest of her life. It would be all over. And that was... that's what she wanted, right? That would be good.

"But you couldn't even read them before," Alice said. Maybe going slowly wasn't so bad. She knew she should try to fix Wonderland sooner but...

"Maybe I can now, though. It's been a while. This evening you can show me and we can try."

"This evening," Alice agreed, though she was less sure she wanted help anymore.

CHAPTER 11

First Step

THE ONSLAUGHT OF homework kept Alice from having to walk Adrianna through any of the books or teach her anything. Alice made sure she was always much too busy with something to give her a hand, pushing back the time they would start and promising it would come eventually.

She didn't know why she was so hesitant. Maybe it wouldn't be as bad as she feared. Help would be good. Having Adrianna actually there to help her and understand what was going on would only be good. She could finally have someone who understood everything. And yet, she still hesitated.

The whole thing was giving her a headache that wouldn't go away. It was harder and harder to sleep. Alice blamed it on stress and worry over what was going to happen when she showed up at Combat Club today. Heather didn't want to talk to her. In the best case, Heather would ignore her. Her mind ran through the worst cases where she might decide to make Alice pay for showing up. This was probably a bad idea, but Adrianna was insistent. Even Sarah thought it would be good if she went.

Alice headed to Combat Club, leaving Adrianna to continue sleeping. She'd given up trying to figure out how to print her permission slip and just forwarded the slip over to the people in charge. It took her a while to remember that Tasha wasn't there any longer, now off at university like Lori. Alice felt like she was coming in too late in the year, but there were tryouts this morning for people who wanted to join.

Alice joined the lineup and did her laps, glancing around to see if there were any people here she knew. Heather was lingering somewhere in the background, not paying any attention to her. She had been seen, she knew, and Heather was watching her through the introductions to the laps, talking with Adam between glances. Peter was there as well, preparing his station. In the stands, Lance was watching.

It wasn't until they were told to start going through the stations when she noticed that Arthur had also decided to show up. He appeared next to her, grinning and looking her over. "If it isn't the witch," he said. "Combat isn't the place for little girls who get tricked by monsters."

"I won, didn't I?" Alice asked, no pride or joy in her

voice. "You aren't in his garden. Can you do this with only one hand?"

Arthur itched at his prosthetic, glaring down at her. "There isn't a person here who can best me, even with this... handicap." He frowned as he said it, clearly unhappy with the word choice, and he let Alice take the lead.

Heather was in charge of the first station. Arthur let Alice go first, walking around to hold the punching bag, watching and waiting for her to do something impressive. Alice tried a few hits, aware that Heather's eyes were on her as well. She wasn't doing anything unusual, but Alice knew she was holding back, nervous under the eyes of two people.

"Cat," Heather said.

Alice drew her hand back but she just couldn't hit as hard at the sound of his name anymore. After everything, he wasn't worth the ire.

"Does she hate cats, now?" Arthur asked, amusement playing on his face.

"Before your time," Heather told him. "Alice attracts the worst people."

"Does that make you one of the worst?" Arthur asked, a grin on his face.

Amusement played over Heather's face, but she turned back to Alice, nodding for her to continue. Alice punched again, trying to ignore everything happening around her. She wasn't sure if it was better or worse that Heather was acknowl-edging her presence.

"You really are awful at this," Arthur noted. He took a step closer to Alice and gave one of her feet a kick, knocking her off balance as he let out a click with his tongue. "You don't even know how to *stand* right. How do you expect to be of any use?"

Alice didn't see what happened while she got to her feet, only that Heather had left her spot observing them and grabbed Arthur by his existing wrist before he could do any-thing else. Heather pulled him away and gave him a shove to move on. "Next station," she told him, warning.

Arthur looked her carefully over before moving on. He didn't seem to think Heather should have done that or any-thing at all, but Alice was grateful that he wasn't planning to do anything about it. At least, not right now.

"Sorry," Alice said.

"For what?" Heather demanded. When Alice didn't say anything, she pressed, "Really, tell me what you're sorry for."

Alice was very sure that she was looking for a specific answer. She watched her, trying to come up with whatever answer she was looking for. "I can go," she said instead. "This is your thing, I—"

"Oh no you don't," she said, guiding her back to the

punching bag. "You need this place more than I do and we both know it. Go."

Alice hesitated before landing a punch. And another. Heather didn't look impressed and Alice could feel Heather's eyes burning into her, but she tried not to let it get to her.

"I'm going to talk," Heather said. "Look. I get that you're stressed about all the shit that's been happening and that keeps happening to you. I get it. But if someone tries to help you, you don't just yell at them and leave. *You take the damn hand.* And you stop lying about shit. It's not like we can't see that you're having problems."

"I'm fine," Alice said. This time, she landed it well and the bag jumped in Heather's hands.

"If you're fine, then I don't need this scholarship anymore," Heather said. "You want to deal with it on your own, fine. Just don't expect anyone else to feel bad for you when it all goes to shit. I'm done trying to help you."

"Okay," Alice said. She couldn't quite get the punch as solidly this time.

Alice wanted to say more, but she knew better. Defending herself would only make it worse. It was better to stay very quiet and make her think that she agreed. Her mind worked on a way to agree without actually agreeing to anything. Her head was already pounding and she wasn't sure how much more of this she would be able to deal with.

Heather seemed to accept this, at least for now. "Next station," she said. "Maybe get a drink first. You look a little pale."

Alice walked past Arthur to get a water bottle from the table, watching as he drew a crowd as he sparred with Adam. Her feet slowed as she watched, seeing Arthur handle a wooden sword with a grimace on his face and his left arm tucked behind his back. Still, Adam was sweating and, though he wasn't losing, he didn't seem to be able to keep the upper hand for long.

She wondered where Arthur had learned that. In Adam's movements, Alice could see shades of Tiger Lily and the Mad Hatter, but Arthur was different. His face was frozen in concentration, brows knitted and sweat beading on his forehead, and his left arm twitched behind him with every strike. He didn't move as much, didn't have the same flourish or drama and relied more on carefully chosen direct hits that Adam was too fast to be caught with. They were largely short and sharp movements, precise and no more than necessary, more power than theater.

She wondered again where he had come from. Something about this was worrying her.

She kept moving, going to where Peter was. He was showing people the easy way to grab people and get out of holds, much like he'd practiced with Alice. When she appeared, he pranced over and grabbed Alice by the arm. "Finally," he said, tugging her to the front of his small audience. "Someone who knows what they're doing! Are you okay? You look awful."

"It's fine," Alice said. Her head was pounding, but she could still feel Heather keeping an eye on her. She was going to at least try to make it through this. She took a steadying breath, put her water bottle down next to the boy Peter had been using as an example.

Now that she was looking, Peter didn't look so great either. There were circles under his eyes, but he was still smiling like they were sneaking in to use the gym instead of using it as it was intended. She lowered her voice. "No flying," she told Peter quietly.

"No disappearing," he told her with a grin and a wink, bringing her to the front. "Okay, this is how it's done!"

There were only a handful of people here to watch what they were doing. The boy Peter had been using to show them what to do went back to take a seat, looking pityingly at Alice as she was dragged up in front of them and looking back at Peter. He rubbed his arm and mouthed a warning to Alice to be careful.

Peter didn't give her a chance to prepare before he was on her, Alice narrowly managing to dodge her way around him. Her head was pounding and making her slow, not able to get out of the way fast enough a second time before he grabbed her by the arm and started to twist it back behind her.

All of a sudden, Peter stopped his attack and looked around. "Do you hear that?" he asked. His eyes were haunted, like when he thought or talked about Neverland. "It sounds like Hook's cannons."

"I don't hear anything," said someone sitting in front of them.

Alice squeezed her eyes shut and didn't see who it was. Her head was pounding louder now, the sharp pain coming from the very back of her mind and making her want very much to lie down. Would it be rude to take a nap in front of these people? Or would they be rude for becoming an audience to it?

"Are you—"

The pain that flared through her head was blinding. She had never felt anything like it before, all-encompassing and like the back of her skull had just shattered into a hundred tiny pieces. Her eyes flew open and she saw a flash of white, followed by a flash of something very wrong. She was certain whatever she was looking at, if she was looking at anything at all, wasn't happening there. Something was happening somewhere else. Darkness and light and something swirling together, mixing into something new and wrong and strangely right.

She heard a scream and it wasn't hers. Hers was caught in her throat and she choked on it as Peter's voice rang out loud. As the world went dark, she saw Peter drop to the ground and she followed.

CHAPTER 12

Decoration Choices

OH NO, THIS would not do at all. Alice was *most* disappointed with these accommodations. The white linens and the white curtains and the white walls were simply plain and hardly something that they should be tolerating, no matter *how* much their tuition cost. *Especially* with how much their tuition cost, now that she thought of it.

"This will not do at all," Alice muttered, looking around. She sat up slowly, taking in the rest of her surroundings. She was not alone in this room, instead it was filled with people and many of those people had eyes that were looking at her, coming closer to her, saying things that she couldn't quite hear through the dim ringing in her ears.

"If someone would be so kind, please shut off whatever is making that sound," she told them, watching as Heather got closer and tried to push her back down to the bed. "I'm afraid

I can't hear a thing you're saying, but I assure you that I'm quite all right," she insisted. "I do hope you all haven't been watching me sleep. That's terribly rude to not tell me you'd be observing me. None of you have gotten such permission, written or otherwise, I assure you."

"This is boring!" came Peter's voice, cutting through the ringing in her ears. Even he was rubbing at his ears, but he leapt up in the air in protest. He hung there, turning on Alice and bending down at the hip, hands in fists resting on his thighs. His face came close enough that she could see each strand of his dark hair falling into his darker eyes. "No one cares about writing stuff down for you, Alice!"

Alice got to her feet, looking back up at him and poking him in the forehead to make him back away. "Perhaps you should! Haven't your parents taught you anything? You do have a father now, don't you?"

"Wiggles isn't the boss of me!" Peter said. "I'm Peter Pan! *No one* can tell me what to do! The fairies said so!"

"This is what Lily was talking about," Adam muttered.

"She hasn't said a word to me about it!" Alice exclaimed, shocked as she turned to Adam. Peter was forgotten while he rubbed his head. "Do tell, has she said much about me? I should think she would know better than to gossip. She seems so sensible."

"I can't blame her for not saying anything," Arthur said. "You've gone completely mental."

"How can you tell?" Lance said, a grin on his face and a laugh in his words.

Alice ignored the shock on Adam's face as Lance and Arthur laughed amongst themselves. Alice would not stand for this at all! "I will have you know," Alice insisted, storming over to the pair of them, "I may be mental, but at least I have the manners to know that you do not intrude on a sleeping person. Perhaps you were seeking another kiss while I wasn't paying attention? Or did you think I forgot about that particular incident?" She raised her eyebrows defiantly, though Arthur was still laughing at her. Rude.

"Gross!" Peter threw his hands up and flipped upside down in the air. "Why do you gotta keep on about the boring stuff? We could be doing something *fun* right now. Does the lake have mermaids?"

"Why's he— *How* is— Why didn't anyone tell me he could *fly?*" Heather finally said, settling on a question after all that sputtering.

"Well, you never asked," Alice informed her. It was obvious really. "If you expect an answer, you must ask a question. Terribly rude to expect anyone to know what you are talking about otherwise." Alice got up and appeared in front of Heather. "And you used to be so sensible, Heather. A shame to see you fall to such terrible habits. Perhaps you should think before you speak. Or perhaps you should return to silence. Nothing unfortunate can be said if nothing is said at all."

Heather balked and backed into the bed. "What's going on?" she demanded.

"Oh, far too much," Alice said, looking around the room and taking everything into account. "Just to begin with, I would say some terrible decorating practices are at work. Much too much white. A little colour would do this room no harm. There's no reason to have so much *nothing*."

"Oh, Lily talked about this too," Adam muttered.

"What does your ex have to do with this?" Heather snapped at him. "Why are you okay with this?"

"*Not to mention*," Alice pressed, glaring at him. So rude, interrupting her like that. "There are far too many people in here. I daresay, I hope you weren't all here just to watch me sleep. Not only is it a terribly dull thing to watch, but also very upsetting that you would not inform me that I was meant to amuse you first. And you didn't even ask if I was prepared for such a performance!"

"We weren't—"

"*Don't*," Adam warned Heather.

"What is this?" Heather's eyes were wide and her voice low as she clung to Adam. "Why aren't you freaking out?"

"She does have a point," Arthur said. His eyes narrowed on Heather. "Far too many people in here."

His good arm passed through the air and Heather shrank in size. Her gym clothes melted into her and she grew fur, her excited yelp morphing quickly into panicked trilling. Her dark skin sprouted a mix of light and dark fur, her grabbing fingers shrinking into clawed paws scratching at Adam's side. Adam jumped back, watching in horror as Heather turned into a very scared raccoon.

"What are you doing?" Lance snapped at Arthur. "You can't just..."

"Don't go losing your backbone now," Adam told him, but his attention was squarely on the raccoon now trying to claw its way up his leg.

While Adam was asking something about rabies shots and Peter's laughter fluttered through the air, Alice appeared in front of Arthur, frowning deeply. Next to him, Lance's face had gone blank, but that wasn't a problem. He didn't really understand what the issue was anyway. "That wasn't very polite," Alice scolded Arthur. "I was going to ask what she thought of the curtains, but now you've made her colour blind!"

"Not the time!" Adam yelled back at her.

"Of course it is!" Alice said, turning back on him. She took one step over and appeared on his other side, putting him between herself and Heather's incessant trilling. "I was just about to make some *polite conversation* and hopefully rees-tablish a dialogue with Heather. We haven't been talking, you see, and this seemed like a good time to mutually commiserate over the drab decor. Given how colourful her notebooks are, I assumed she would have some input on how to improve it. And with her connections, perhaps those plans could be given action! But I suppose that will just have to wait, won't it?"

"You have no idea how much I hate you right now." He wasn't looking at her anymore and managed to grab Heather. She shook and writhed in his outstretched hands, clawing them so hard that blood appeared in the scratches.

"You appear to be bleeding," Alice said. "Be careful, it looks like that might get on something. If everything weren't so white it would be a lot easier to clean up, but unfortunately…"

"Let her go!" Peter laughed. "Give her a sword! Can she still fight? Can I fight a raccoon?"

"*No*," Adam said. "I swear, whatever you did to her, if you don't put her back…"

"And if I don't put your little handmaid back, you will do nothing," Arthur informed him. "Perhaps you'd like to join her?"

"Arthur don…" Again, Lance trailed off, looking off in the distance for only a moment before a smile flickered across his face. "So long as it doesn't leave this room it would be pretty funny."

Peter let out a long, exaggerated sigh, bending over backward in the air until he looped around and swooped in next to Alice. "Alice! Come on, let's have an adventure. This place is boring."

"Quite unfortunate," Alice agreed, looking around. There were still far too many people in here and now there was even a wild animal. And from the more and more agitated trilling, and from how she flailed and scratched Adam, Alice was very certain that she was wild. "And possibly a fire code violation. Terrible etiquette, so many people being in here. And even a possible need for animal control now! I do believe about three of you are just going to have to leave."

Peter's shadow appeared to stick his tongue out at her while Peter bent over at the waist and stared her down as he hovered over her. "Who cares if there's a fire? Stop being dumb and come *on!* We can find pirates!"

"I will *not* come on!" Alice snapped back at him. He was terribly rude and inconsiderate and she was not going to tolerate such a thing. "You must learn to understand that safety is an important matter, and especially in such a small place. Why, what if something were to happen and we couldn't escape! We wouldn't be able to find enough tea for all these people!"

"*Ugh,*" Peter groaned. "Then maybe they can make it

pretty or whatever and you can stop being so *boring*. Come on, we're going to have an adventure!" He swooped down to grab her, his shadow matching his movements and somehow looking much more menacing as he did.

"If I've told you once, it's already been too many times!" Alice snapped back at him, taking a step away from him and appearing behind him. He stopped before he collided into Adam and Heather, now scurrying away under one of the beds. He rounded back on Alice as she glared back at him and wagged a finger in his face. "You will *not* be carrying me through the air again! It's much too uncomfortable and you are a terrible transportation device."

"Girls are stupid anyway!" he snapped back at her.

"At least I know what India is!" Alice snapped back, aghast.

"Maybe just sit down, both of you," Adam suggested. He was, as Alice predicted, now bleeding on the white surroundings and about to leave a stain. She had warned him, and he had clearly not listened. No one knew when to listen to her.

"Oh, I will *not* be staying!" Alice insisted. She went to the window that had been showing the forest outside, but now Wonderland was the only thing there. "A good day to you all!"

She took a step into the mirror and the fatigue hit her all at once. She collapsed into the other side of the mirror and let Wonderland swallow her up.

CHAPTER 13

Summons

HER HEAD WAS still buzzing when she awoke on the couch. Something still felt very wrong, but at least it didn't hurt quite as much anymore. She looked around to find the inside of the White Rabbit's house, though the large ears and eyes that loomed over her were not his.

"Hello," she said to the March Hare. "I do hope that you know that watching someone sleep is quite rude."

"Indeed it is!" the March Hare told her brightly, looking much happier now that she was conscious. "But there is no better way than watching to know when you have awoken. And I should note that I was kind enough to not arouse you prematurely."

"A small comfort," Alice muttered as she swung her legs over the edge of the couch.

"And I did attempt to make you more comfortable!" he

added. "It was a kindness, I think, to move you off of that dirty floor and onto this couch. Almost a bed with how little you are! At least *I* didn't just walk over you and leave!"

Alice glanced back at the mirror, already not liking where this was going. Her eyes narrowed and she looked back up at him. "Why would you do that?" she asked.

"*I* would never!" the March Hare insisted, looking offended. "I just said *I* didn't! You really must learn to listen better, Alice. Very inconsiderate to not."

"Did someone else, then?" she asked. He was already starting to say something and she cut him short. "There must be a reason we are speaking about this right now. Did many people walk over me?"

"Why yes," he said, as if he were only just remembering. "There were *two* young men who decided that they would walk right over you and go out. Not even a word to me! Not so much as a greeting or a pardon for their interruption! You bring the very worst people with you when you come here. Perhaps you should consider more civilized company. Though I do suppose like draws like..."

Alice frowned and got to her feet. Her head was pounding, but there wasn't anything she could do about that now. She wasn't sure which two were here, but she was going to have to fetch them back. Wonderland was not a nice place anymore and she couldn't have them losing their hearts or getting too in love with the place. She hoped it wasn't Adam.

"Did they look alike?" she asked.

"Well," the March hare pondered. His large foot tapped, pounding hard against the floor. "They did both have eyes," he said. "Eyes and noses. Mouths as well that they most certainly didn't know how to use!"

Alice took a slow breath in and let it out. "Did they have the same colour hair?"

"Oh no, not at all."

That told her very little, she realized, and she got to her feet. "Thank you very much. You've been most helpful. If you'll excuse me, I must take my leave—"

"Oh, I have nearly forgotten!" Hare said, reaching into his pocket. He pulled out a piece of paper, handing it to her. "I have been sent to deliver this to you when you returned. Very important, most urgent."

"I am not staying long," Alice warned him.

"I should hope not!" Hare said. "You are needed very much elsewhere."

Alice looked back down at the note and frowned. She didn't know the handwriting, but there was a flourish to it that made it look like an invitation. The heading on it didn't help, though it was written on a scrap.

You are cordially invited!

The Queen of Hearts has seen fit to ram her castle through that hole in the universe. You are invited to attend the attempt to keep anything from coming through now that she had created a very large hole. Terrible things on the other side, I must say. Awful manners. Very dangerous. You must meet us on the front lines.

Bring crumpets. This is not optional.

The Mad Hatter

It was exactly the kind of thing she would expect from the Mad Hatter. She went to the White Rabbit's kitchen and looked through the cupboard until she found a small collection of crumpets and a bag to put them in. If it was that bad, she was not going to waste time with arguing.

"I do hope you've gotten permission before deciding to rummage through another person's things!" The March Hare looked aghast, but Alice wasn't perturbed as she looked for jam. She wasn't about to let the Mad Hatter be distracted by anything.

"Will you be coming?" Alice asked instead, settling the bag on her back and preparing to go. She hoped one of the two she had to retrieve was Peter. If it was, he could get back on his own. She really hoped the other wasn't Adam or he'd never go back.

"Oh no," Hare said. "I am only meant to go. Returning is much more a matter for my partner."

Alice nodded and turned away. "Thank you for your hospitality," she said. "I must be off. It seems there is a front line I must tend to."

"Terribly rude things, front lines," Hare said.

Alice stepped away and into the forest, intent on heading straight for the castle. Despite the pounding, her head felt strange and she was oddly calm like she hadn't been in a very long time. She tried not to think about it.

The frontlines weren't quite what Alice was expecting. She stopped at the edge, looking out over the field and wondering just what she *was* expecting. From the letter, it sounded like there should have been creatures from Neverland pouring through the hole between Wonderland and Neverland.

Then again, the letter never technically stated that there was anything coming through.

It was too orderly, the lines in front of the castle in a very strict formation and holding very firm. The people against were too small in number, including not many of Tiger Lily's tribe and not enough people from Wonderland, but it didn't seem that the people at the line were doing anything but defend the castle. After a moment of watching, Alice noted that they hadn't taken a step forward.

The fighting was almost quiet in the background as Alice

approached the table at the edge of Tiger Lily's village. There weren't as many from Wonderland fighting back now, more of them taking a break in the field or retreating back to their homes with very little in the way of harm done to them.

It was obvious why to Alice. The problem was not the people defending the castle. They didn't advance at all, simply keeping people away from the castle. Breaking through them was not going to resolve anything. The trouble was the castle itself.

There, embedded into the sky and vanishing part way through, was a wall of the Queen's castle. It tore a hole in the air that extended down to the ground, showing a land that Alice realized had become perpetually night, filled with dark shadows and ominous shapes. It seemed like a poor choice, giving the shambling zombies now creeping out through the tear no chance to adjust to the daylight of Wonderland before they were thrust into it. Very inconsiderate.

"I hope you've remembered the crumpets," The Mad Hatter said, staring at the castle. Behind him, the Jabberwocky slept, not aroused by Alice's presence. It was a strange thing, though Alice couldn't tell why. "I am quite in need of something to eat. Perhaps it will help with this conundrum."

Alice took the bag of crumpets out of her bag and put them down with the jam for the Mad Hatter to inspect. Tiger Lily looked disapprovingly at her until she looked behind her.

"You have brought company, Alice of Wonderland. Were you aware?"

Looking back, Alice saw two people emerging out of the woods behind her. Arthur had his left hand held in his right like it might be a weapon, though Alice doubted the prosthetic could do much. Even Arthur seemed to know that, considering just how annoyed he looked. Behind him, Lance had a grin on his face and let out a small laugh, waving to Alice and urging Arthur onward.

"I was not," Alice told her.

"That is not Adam."

"Lance."

"The one who tried to kill you."

"Yeah," Alice said. "He hasn't done that again."

"You are too trusting."

"You tried to kill me too," Alice pointed out.

"This is hardly the time to talk about killing people!" The Mad Hatter snapped back at them, gesturing at the castle in front of him. "We have a battle on our hands. One that I must say has me baffled."

"They aren't trying to attack us," Tiger Lily told him, turning her back on Alice and leaning across the table to stare at him. "We don't need to be sending anyone into danger if they do not intend to fight."

"Yes, that's been *established*," the Mad Hatter said. "But

just because there's not fighting to be *had* doesn't mean that they should all just *leave*. There is still quite the fight to be had, it's just a different one than we have anticipated. We must turn our attention to the castle."

"The building?" Alice asked.

"Clearly, the castle is the offending force here," he said as if it were obvious. "Even the Jabberwocky is too small to properly engage it in battle. Perhaps if the Duchess' castle hadn't been destroyed we could attempt to convince it to engage, but that's not possible."

"There's another castle," Alice said, looking up in the sky. There was a single cloud far away and she pointed it out. "That cloud has a castle."

"Oh no," the Mad Hatter insisted. "Rude, all of them. Constantly shouting. No concept of stealth or diplomacy. Perhaps we simply keep watching it and keep it from getting any further into the other side. It does look quite terrible there."

"Things are already coming through," Tiger Lily said. "We cannot permit anything else to come in because of your reckless Queen."

"Is that the Jabberwocky?" Arthur demanded. He was breathless as he got close, staring wide eyed as he drew close enough. The Jabberwocky did not stir, continuing to sleep despite how red in the face Arthur was as he got closer. He turned on Alice. "You just couldn't keep yourself from releasing the most dangerous creatures, could you?"

"To be honest," Alice told him, "I only intentionally released the Jabberwocky. The rest simply decided that they would come along as well. I can hardly be blamed for whatever else decided to invite themselves along with him."

"What have you *done* to it?" Arthur demanded, getting closer. "It took three men to take down that and you have it sleeping like some common dog!"

"I'd consider it an uncommon dog," Alice noted.

"*Most* uncommon," the Mad Hatter said, looking Arthur over as he rose. "I daresay he's probably not even a dog. And who, might I ask, are you? Terribly rude to approach a meeting without so much as a pardon!"

Arthur scowled at him, but relaxed. "Arthur Pendragon," he said. "*King* Arthur Pendragon. And what is that?"

"That is a castle," Hatter said, looking concerned. "Have you never seen one before? I would think a King would be more familiar with this sort of architecture."

"What is it *doing?*"

"Continuing to be a castle," Hatter said, turning back to Alice. "Your friends never seem to be very bright. Though I suppose there may be a reason for that."

"The castle rammed into Neverland," Alice explained to him. "I'd very much like it removed. It's giving me quite the headache when I'm at school and I'm afraid it's a thoroughly ghastly sight. That is hardly a place for a castle. No landscaping at all. How did it get there in the first place?"

Hatter looked uncomfortable, but Tiger Lily was quick to respond. "They decided to take tea," she said, not looking at Hatter. "And they did not make us aware so that we could take a turn."

"Every day at the same time!" Hatter cried. "You should know by now."

"There is no *time* here," Tiger Lily insisted. "You have no sun that sets, no moon that rises, no way to tell when time passes."

"We have tea! That is as clear a marker as the sun!"

Alice was forgotten as soon as they started in on one another in an argument that sounded like they had it rehearsed. Instead, her attention drifted to the two people she was supposed to bring back to school with her as they wandered across the field to the castle. In a step, she strode next to Lance while he trailed behind Arthur.

"Hey," she said. "Where you going?"

"Arthur is going to try to take the castle," Lance told her. There was something about him that was far too calm. It was like he had been taking lessons from Adam with how he sounded almost excited about getting directly involved in a Wonderland fight.

"Will you come back?" she asked. "Or is this going to be like Adam and I'm going to need to get Tiger Lily involved?"

Lance let out a laugh. "I doubt it," he said. "Arthur wouldn't take orders from her. He just needs to get this out of his system. He's been a bit out of sorts. The school isn't his home, you know. None of this is either. And he is no longer the man he went to sleep as. It's been very jarring. He's very lost and still trying to figure out what he should be doing with himself. A castle raid is something familiar, though I suspect he will give it up as soon as he realizes that this one is going to be very different than what he's used to."

He smiled and looked back at her. "Not to worry," he assured her. "I'll make sure he returns. Just allow him this."

Something nagged at her, that these were not words that Lance would say, but the content of the phrase was enough to satisfy her for now. Arthur was far ahead of them now, demanding something from one of the troops and growing angry as the man didn't move. He grabbed the hilt of the sword out of the man's scabbard and struggled to pull it out.

Above him, coming to sit on top of the castle, Alice spotted another small boy watching. He curled up and Alice remembered what the Hare said. Two had walked over her. He didn't mention any others, but if Peter had flown, he would not be included.

"So long as you promise to come back," Alice said. "I'll

be back for both of you shortly." With that, she took another step and vanished.

CHAPTER 14

Passing on Neverland

IT WAS A beautiful chaos from the parapet. Night and day mingled in strange, lazy circles, battling in the center for dominance. Stars dotted the daylight in small bursts of orange and blue to fight their way through the blue sky while the sun insisted on shining down into the forest of Neverland, lighting up nothing. It felt so wrong, but there was something beautiful about it and she couldn't look away.

"You made it," Peter said quietly next to her.

Alice sat down next to him on the parapet and watched him. He wasn't small as he watched Neverland, not scared like he usually was. He just looked tired.

They stared out into Neverland, into the moving shadows and the forest that looked even larger and more dense than the last time Alice had seen it. Things kept moving in and out of the trees and none of them were small. Many of them looked too close to human for comfort, and there was no telling how dangerous any of them were as they started creeping closer.

"I don't want to do this anymore," he told her. "This isn't fun anymore. I don't think it's been fun for a while."

Alice took a slow breath in next to him. The air from Neverland drifted across and it felt colder than Wonderland. "Was it ever fun?"

Peter nodded. "It used to be. When it was just me and the Lost Boys. We played all day and they would come and then I'd kill them when they got too old. But that was a game too. I just let them go back." He perked up just a little. "There used to be day in Neverland. It didn't used to be night. There were pirates and unicorns and Indians. But I guess I'm not supposed to call them Indians."

"That's racist," Alice agreed. She kept looking up to see where Wonderland was fighting back, spiralling and swirling the lighter blues of the sky into the darkness of Neverland. The movements were almost relaxing, each advance and retreat matching the pulsing and pounding in her mind. "Can you feel that?"

Peter nodded and said nothing for a while. Below them, the sounds of a fight were only just beginning, too faint to know what was really going on. Neither of them looked. "It's not going to stop," he told her. "Not as long as I'm whatever I am to Neverland. But…"

Alice gave him a moment, but he didn't finish. "Is it Wendy?" she asked.

"I shouldn't have brought her," he said. "I thought it was because she was a girl, but you didn't destroy Wonderland when you got a book. Kevin thinks I pushed her too far. We didn't let her do anything but get kidnapped and tell us stories. We didn't let her play with us. He said that can drive a person insane."

"You told Kevin?"

"He's my brother now," Peter said. "More than the Lost Boys were. They never told me when I was wrong. They just agreed with me no matter what I told them. I don't know if they were even friends really. They were just... They did anything I said. Now people tell me when I'm being stupid or mean. They get mad at me. I think I'm actually getting older."

"That's how time works." Alice wasn't sure what he was talking about, but she didn't know if she wanted another silence so soon. She needed to carry her weight in this conversation.

"Not in Neverland," Peter said. "Sometimes the Lost Boys would get younger before they got older. I don't know how long I've been there, but Wiggles has grown up a lot. And there have been a lot of Lost Boys that have come and gone since him. Every time I went into the world to find more, it changed more, but I was always the same."

"And now?"

"I'm older most of the time. But sometimes, when I hear the cannons, I get very young again inside. It's like I'm a little kid again. But Neverland is more like my nightmares than my dreams now. Isn't that what Wonderland is like?"

It was Alice's turn to go quiet as she thought about it. "I don't think Wonderland is just mine," she said. "I think other people came before me and more people will come when I'm done. If it's still here. It didn't let me back in for years. It wasn't until Cat came for me a few years ago that I got to see it again."

"You're scared it won't let you back after you do everything?"

Alice hesitated. She didn't like that there were words for what she was feeling. She really didn't like that someone had actually said them out loud.

"Is that a bad thing?"

Thoughts of a life without Wonderland came to mind. Her parents still together and Lori living at home because they hadn't wasted her childhood with arguing and with doctors. Friends who weren't mad at her because of Wonderland. Good grades, a great college, a real future that included all the things her father wanted for her. A husband. Children. A house with one of those fences people liked.

Yes, that was what she should want.

Peter kept staring into Neverland, though he wasn't really looking at it. He let out a breath at the end, his shoulders slumping before his back went very straight. He rose off the parapet, not looking back at Alice. "I think it's time I grew up. Can you come with me?"

"Lead the way," Alice told him.

THERE WAS SOMETHING different about going through Neverland with Peter this time. The forest was very aware of both of them as they walked through it and it was making the trip a lot easier for Peter. There were fewer low-hanging branches in his path as he flew along next to Alice,

"Why does it all move for you?" Alice asked, narrowly missing tripping on a fallen branch. Around them, she could see dark shadows moving that turned away as soon as they might have been an issue.

"I think Neverland knows," he said. "I abandoned it. Now it wants to make it easy for me to go."

"That's awfully rude of it."

"It's not like I want it anyway!"

"Still terrible manners." Alice shut her mouth and held her jaw closed. What sort of manners was she expecting a world to have? Something felt off about that. "Where are we going?"

"Someone took over the Lost Boys," Peter said. "He will take Neverland off my hands if I ask."

"Have you been coming back? How do you know?"

Peter let his silence speak for him. Alice wasn't sure what to make of it. He always seemed too scared of Neverland, and he had been much better about attending classes and not disappearing all weekend like Alice had. It was strange to think that he'd also been disappearing without her knowing. Maybe he'd been gone at the same times she was.

"I don't sleep much anymore," he said finally. "Maybe after this... Oh, right there."

Without waiting for her, Peter swept up into the branches and took a seat. He let out a loud sound, one that Alice knew was supposed to sound like a crow though she didn't think it sounded much like anything at all. Still, she went to join him at the base of the tree and kept her eyes out at the dark trees around her for some sign of something dangerous approaching. Or for this other person he talked about.

There were eyes watching soon, but none of them came out. Alice was ready to run, but Peter said nothing, floating down to the ground next to her and leaning against the trunk. He was much too calm given that this was Neverland. Past the eyes, Alice could see wolves roaming, and she remembered far too well what the wolves here were like.

"*No girls!*" came a voice from the bushes. "You know the ru— Oh, is that Alice?"

A boy of no more than eight came out of the bushes, dark hair and fair skin, mischievous brown eyes peering at Alice. As his face lit up, Alice realized who this boy was, and she wasn't nearly as excited to see him in his intentionally tattered Lucena Academy uniform as he was to see her. "You're not supposed to be here!"

"Matt?" Alice asked. She opened her mouth to say more, but her words were a jumble in her mind and she shut it again. Now that he was still and Alice was in her right mind, she could tell why Matt was so hard to find. Not only had he been hiding in Neverland, but he was a much younger boy than the one that went through the mirror. Her words failed her.

Peter didn't have the same issue, pushing off of the tree and stepping between them. "You said you wanted Neverland, right?" he asked.

"I thought you said it was yours," Matt said. "You made it, right?"

"I changed my mind. Do you want it or not? I think Samson said he would take it if you didn't."

Alice looked around at the darkness, spotting a pair of eyes as they scurried away from Matt's cutting glare back at them. They had quite an audience watching from the shadows, but this was all happening so quickly. Surely it wasn't this easy to be done with it.

"I want it," Matt said. "How do we do this?"

"Give me your knife."

That statement and the ease with which Matt pulled one out from his pocket snapped Alice back to the present. She should stop this. She didn't know the person was Matt, the one Case brother that she had been unable to find until now. It was her fault that he was stuck here in the first place, her fault that their family was now short one member.

But looking at him now, watching as he hesitated to hand the knife over, he was not the boy that had fallen through the mirror all those years ago. He was half the age he'd been when he disappeared and missed years of school to fight zombies. She didn't know if he could ever catch up now, or if anyone would even believe he was the same boy who had gone missing all those years ago.

In front of her, Peter finally snatched the knife out of Matt's hand and sliced his palm open before handing it back to Matt and instructing him to do the same. Matt didn't hesitate, didn't even flinch as he cut open his own hand before flipping the knife back into his pocket, still dripping with their blood.

Peter held out his hand. It was about to happen.

"Wait," Alice said. She had to at least talk to him. Tell

him he had an option. "Matt. Do you want to come back? Because if you do this, you might never get to go back."

Matt's jaw set and his eyes stayed on Alice as he thrust his hand into Peter's. "I don't ever wanna go back," he said. "Never."

Alice wasn't sure what she was expecting, but nothing happened. She watched as they shook hands, Peter towering over Matt, his dark hand so much larger than Matt's tiny pale one. There was no light, no feeling of something immense happening, no ground shaking around her. The forest didn't cry out, didn't rumble, didn't even send a breeze past them. Not even the Lost Boys hiding in the bushes did anything. It was, for all Alice could tell, only a handshake and nothing more.

"Hey? If you see her, tell Wendy I'm sorry," Peter said.

Matt made a sour face. "Tell her yourself. I'm gonna run this place now, right? I don't have to do anything for you."

Peter looked okay with this and he drew his bloody hand back. Staring at it, he frowned and looked down at his shirt. He grabbed a fist full of the white material in his hand and it bloomed red as his hand continued to bleed into it.

"Is that it?" Matt asked, looking at his own hand. He pulled out his knife again and cut off some of his already torn pants to tie around his hand. "I don't feel any different."

"That's it," Peter said. A bright smile appeared on his face and he floated up off the ground. "Good luck."

Matt didn't look impressed.

"I gotta go do some *real* stuff. Bye Alice. Tell Addie to stop being dumb."

Alice watched him disappear into the forest. It all seemed too easy. There had to be a catch. Something beyond Peter's bleeding hand, one that he was now wrapping up with the loose bit of his shirt. Still, when Peter started to drift off into the forest, she followed behind him, watching to see if there really was anything at all that had happened.

Peter looked like a weight had been lifted. She hadn't noticed before, but the way he flew had even changed. Whatever tether was keeping him from enjoying the experience was gone and he fluttered through the smaller loops in the trees. He was calm in those lazy loops. The stress that Alice had ignored for these years, that she thought was a normal feature of his face, were gone.

Part of her envied him.

"Better?" she asked as they went back through the forest.

"*So much*," he said. "I can't hear the cannons anymore. Or anything else. And I never have to come back again! When we get back, you should find someone to give Wonderland to."

"Let's go through the castle," Alice said. "I can find a mirror for you."

CHAPTER 15

Morgana

DESPITE THE FIGHT that was brewing on the Wonder-land side, there was nothing stopping anyone from walking into the back door of the castle through Neverland and letting themselves in. It was only a matter of time before Wendy's zombies made their way in. For now, though, Alice and Peter headed into the small back door and found themselves in a grand entrance.

"Wonderland is weird," Peter told her.

"I hope no one expects this to be a proper greeting," Alice said loudly to no one in particular. "A fine entrance room is no substitute for an actual greeting."

"*Shhhh!* You're going to get us caught!"

"It's rude," Alice said. She kept walking and Peter fol-lowed along a few feet off the ground, his eyes darting around for anyone that might hear them. "Not to mention you. Just because you're flying doesn't mean you shouldn't wipe your feet at the door. They are filthy."

"You know this is dumb, right?"

Alice kept her mouth from opening to say whatever the first thing that crossed her mind might be. She was doing it again. Talking like Wonderland. She couldn't keep doing that. "I am aware," Alice said. "I'll try to stop."

There was a crack behind them and Peter snapped around, darting up another several feet into the high ceiling. Alice was annoyed about the fact that something had made a noise without advance warning or so much as a prompt apology. She turned much more slowly, her eyes landing on the woman who had likely caused it.

It took her a moment to recognize her. It was Claudia, Adrianna's stepmother, now dressed in something that looked like it was out of *Lord of the Rings*. "Hello Alice," she said, waving her hand through the air.

A table grew out of the ground between them and she poured three cups of tea, placing two on the other side of the table in front of two chairs that grew out of the carpet. A chair grew for herself as well and she took a seat, her large brown eyes watching them both.

"You look really familiar," Peter said, his eyes darting between Alice and Claudia. "Do we know you?"

"Alice knew a version of me," she said. "She knew me

when I was Claudia Case. I've decided to go back to who I was before. You can call me Morgana."

"Case?" Peter asked, touching back down on the ground. He bent in closer to Alice and asked quietly, "Like Lance and Addie?"

Alice nodded, trying to make herself pay attention and focus. This felt strange and her Wonderland feelings really wanted to take over, but this was not the time. "She's — well, was — their stepmother. You're not going to let us go, are you?"

Claudia — Morgana, Alice supposed — gave her a very gentle smile and waved a hand. She nodded behind Alice. Alice looked back to see a very large mirror behind her. One that, as soon as Alice wanted it to, became a reflection of her room. First the old one, showing two different girls who looked confused at what the mirror was doing, and then turning into her new room.

"Do you still live with Adrianna? Has she mentioned her father at all?" Morgana asked, looking back at the room. Alice didn't say anything turning back to look at her. "You can leave whenever you want," she told Alice. "I am only here to talk. To better understand."

"Adrianna said you were gone," Alice said.

"In a way," Morgana said. She nodded to the tea, but Alice

didn't touch the cup. "I'm having trouble getting answers, Alice."

"It's Wonderland," Alice told her. "The books aren't here."

"Oh, I know," she said. "You've moved them. Protected that friend of yours. I can respect that. I can even respect that you won't give them back. Those are mine, though, don't be mistaken. But," she added, a smile gracing her too red lips, "I may not need them any longer."

"Does that mean you'll stop doing whatever you're doing to me?" she asked. "You're the one who made me not able to put the hearts back, right?"

A pitying laugh echoed in the room and she took a sip of her tea. She looked down on Alice, looking far more patronizing than she had to, like she was trying to explain to a child why they were not allowed to leave. "Magic is much too dangerous to be worked on your own," Morgana said. "It's not safe for you to be reading those books without someone there to guide you."

"That's what I told her!" Peter said. He took a seat at the table to drink the tea and Alice could feel herself moving closer to the table as well.

"I've been fine so far. And I need to put the hearts back." There was something happening in her head and she couldn't figure out what. It was hard to take account of her feelings or come up with a reason to be distrustful of Morgana. She knew she couldn't be trusted, but maybe she could be reasoned with.

Alice tried, but she couldn't remember why Morgana wasn't to be trusted. She remembered her as Claudia buying her ice cream, about her mentioning the corn flavour, but she couldn't remember why she had such misgivings about that day. The more she tried to remember something, the less she came back with. The only thing strange was that she had left her family, but even that was starting to feel less important. Alice took a seat at the table and picked up the tea. "What do you want?"

"Tell me what Neverland is," Morgana pressed. "Wonderland and Neverland. What created them?"

"*I* made Neverland," Peter said. "The fairies brought me there, and it made whatever I wanted. I didn't know for a while, but that's what happened I think."

"Interesting," Morgana said, leaning in her large brown eyes watching him carefully. She took a sip of her tea. "What did you say your name was?"

"Peter."

"Well, Peter, I'd love to hear more. Alice, is that the same way Wonderland was made?"

Something was happening, but Alice couldn't figure out what. Something felt very wrong. The hair on her arms rose. She pinched the inside of her wrist, expecting Morgana to stop her and not sure why. It wasn't a dream, but there was something very wrong here. She put her tea back on the table and looked back at the mirror. Her room was still there. She could just walk away. Morgana wasn't trying to trap her here. She wasn't being held. There was no reason to not believe her.

Alice found herself wanting to stay. She didn't move from her seat or shy away from Morgana's intent brown eyes watching her. Something was wrong, but she didn't know what. And even though she was allowed to leave, she didn't want to. "I don't know," she said, and it was true.

"You must know something."

The more she tried to figure out what was wrong, the less Alice could place the feeling and the more unsettled it made her feel. Which made it a lot harder to force her other impulses away.

"I know that this is not a good place to put a table," Alice told her. "Under a window would be much better, but this room doesn't even have one of those. You would think that an entrance would have a little sunlight. Perhaps some more interesting curtains. Have you thought of finding a new decorator? The red inside this castle is quite overwhelming. I know that the Queen of Hearts has a specific aesthetic, but it wouldn't hurt to try a few different colours!"

From her face, Morgana hadn't been expecting to get such sound decorating advice from her. Alice didn't know why. She didn't do much to affect her surroundings, but she did like them better when they were pretty. Perhaps she didn't know how to *make* them pretty herself, but that was what other people with expertise were for. It was much simpler to point out when one needed redecorating than to do so yourself.

Or perhaps it was rude to point it out. She had been scolded for being rude so often that she didn't know if she cared any longer.

"We can continue this later," Morgana said, rising to her feet. "You two finish your tea. I'll let you know when I need you."

Alice looked at Peter, rolling her eyes as Morgana vanished with a loud crack. "Again, not even a warning that she was going to do that. That sound is much too loud to not apologize."

"You're doing it again," Peter told her.

Alice clenched her jaw and kept her mouth shut. Her head was throbbing. Now that she was paying attention, she could push the Wonderland back and away. Inhaling and exhaling with each pounding of her head, she could get herself under control.

"So if I just walk through that mirror, can I go home?" Peter asked.

Alice looked back at the mirror. It was still her room, still empty. She wondered what time it was and where Adrianna was. Hopefully they had a little more time left before she got back. She needed to find Arthur and Lance and get them all out of there.

"Yeah, I—"

The door clattered open and drew their attention. Lance was standing there, looking wildly around with none of the panic that he usually had in Wonderland. *That* was something that made her worried, more so than the half wooden and half metal sword in his hand that he seemed to actually know how to hold. Something was very wrong here and her alarm bells were going off as he looked back into the hall.

"I found her!" Lance called back into the hall. He let himself in, his head tilting up to Alice in greeting. "Hey Alice. You found Peter!"

"Good timing," Peter said, though he sounded suspicious about it.

Arthur came through the door shortly after him, looking wildly around and his eyes falling on Alice. "You!" he said, storming over to Alice. "What the *hell* is this place?"

"This is an entry hall," Alice told him. "They are pretty common at any enter—"

"*I am not dealing with this right now,*" he told her. He looked back at the door, then cast a very long look at Lance. His shoulders dropped and he deflated. "Get us out of here. Now."

"That isn't a very polite way to make a request."

Arthur looked at her like he might do something. His head suddenly snapped back around at the door, gripping his sword more tightly at his side. From the hall, Alice could hear several heavy feet drawing closer at an alarming pace.

"I will make an exception this time. Through the mirror, everyone."

CHAPTER 16

Magic Class

THERE WAS SOMETHING different about all of them since they got back from Wonderland. She heard that Alice and Peter had an issue when she went to Combat Club and they had both fainted, but somehow that had turned into a trip to Wonderland. Adam told her that much after coming back covered in scratches and looking like he had lost a fight with an animal. He said nothing about which animal, telling her again to stay away from Arthur. As if she had a choice in the matter.

Arthur wasn't hanging over her shoulder anymore, though. The corner of her eye was vacant of the boy that had been following her all semester. She hoped this meant that he had given up at last. He hadn't spoken to her again since that day. When she did see him, it looked like he had made friends with Lance.

She still hadn't talked to Lance. Too much kept happening.

Alice was a greater concern for her. After what she learned about the fight with Heather, the side that Alice could remember and she couldn't, she was watching her more closely. Since her return, she would say strange things sometimes, though caught herself quickly and fell silent. The bathroom now had a constant supply of painkillers and Alice's headache did not go away.

Adrianna needed to help. The endless homework settled into a steady routine and they had adjusted for the onslaught of their coursework. And Alice had done this on her own for long enough already.

Alice sat at her computer, feet folded under her at her desk. She didn't so much use the computer as she peered at it, curled over it like she was using some strange new device that was about to explode at any moment. Adrianna could see when her shoulders were knotted and when they relaxed, and had spent more than one evening watching as they alternated from one state to the next to try to tell how stressed she was. Tonight they were knotted tight and Alice pulled the lid of her laptop quickly at first, then caught herself to close it softy.

Adrianna's eyes flickered to the mirror. More and more often now when Alice's headaches got bad, she could see a glimpse of Wonderland looking back at her. It was only for a moment, but she was sure other people could see it to. Now, there was nothing in the reflection except for Alice. "Everything okay?" she asked.

"Yeah," Alice said.

"How's Rayne?" Her sister was usually a good place to start, and she knew Alice had been talking to her.

"She's good. Still sending me those emails. She just hit A." Alice looked like she might say more, get her shoulders screwed up into a knot. Adrianna waited a breath and they relaxed again. She turned around in her chair, one of her legs slipping out from under her. "How's Adam? He's still pretty scratched up."

"He'll be okay. He said something about a rabies shot, though."

Silence stretched between the two of them and Alice started to turn back to her desk. Adrianna didn't know how to ask what she wanted to ask, but she knew she had to.

"You think I could do it?" Adrianna asked.

"Do what?" Alice asked. The look on her face was complete bewilderment.

"The books," Adrianna continued. She was already this far. "You can't read them, but maybe I could now. It might be worth a try. Maybe I could learn to put the hearts back for you."

"You're not going back to Wonderland," Alice told her.

"It's got Neverland zombies bleeding into it now and they don't even know proper manners or when to stop for tea."

There was the strangeness again. Adrianna looked at her and chose her next words far too carefully for what should be a normal conversation. "If you can't do it, then you're never going to get free of Wonderland, Alice. Tiger Lily couldn't do it, right? And she said you should find someone else. Maybe I can. And I won't go over without you. I can't, right? Peter's not going to take me."

Kevin said Peter had been different since then too. But that was something to ask about another time.

"You won't go crazy reading them?" Alice asked. "Try to take over the school and start stealing hearts?"

"I can't get to the books without you either," she reminded her. She also didn't know where exactly Alice's hand disappeared to when she reached into the air for them. "I couldn't even read them before. I might not be able to read them at all. But if I can, there might be a way that we don't have to worry so much about all of this. And when we figure it out, I can help you finish up everything in Wonderland and you won't have to deal with it anymore."

It was the best way to relieve Alice of all the stress. Without Wonderland, she could focus on getting her life in order here. With Combat Club, Alice wasn't supposed to be going to Wonderland anymore. Hopefully next week, that would be true. They would need to make plans so she was too busy to go through the mirror. A normal weekend would do her good.

"If you can," Alice agreed. She reached into the air and her hand disappeared. It still made Adrianna anxious, not knowing where it went and if it would ever return, but sure enough Alice's arm lowered and her hand reappeared with a large brown book. She handed it to Adrianna before sitting down in front of her bed, watching. "I have some notes if you can do it. They'll probably be easier to work with than the whole book."

Adrianna didn't let her fingers linger on the cover. It felt strange and unsettling in a way she couldn't place. Like it might have once been alive. Like it might still be. She went to the pages, flipping through to find an index of strange creatures she had never seen before. She lingered on a few, ones where the pictures were missing. The Jabberwocky and the Jubjub birds had escaped. She wondered if the other monsters in here were ready to do the same.

"Anything?" Alice asked.

"It's not as interesting as I thought it would be," Adrianna said, glancing through the pages. "It's just a catalog of creatures. I don't know why I thought it would be a full spell book. That's where the Jabberwocky escaped from, isn't it?"

Alice looked over and started to waver on her feet as soon as her eyes hit the page. She blinked slowly and pulled herself away, trying to keep her balance while she caught her breath. "I think so," she said.

"Are you all right?"

Alice nodded and sat down at her desk. "Looks like you can read them," Alice said, opening up her computer. "Which means these might be more useful to you." She started going through her computer, folding her feet under her again. "I tried to take a bunch of notes on the books a while ago," she said. "I think I told you. But there's a few spells that I have worked out. You can try one or two of them, see if they actually work."

"Are you okay with this?" Adrianna asked. This all felt easy, and she wasn't sure if it was because Alice was okay with it or if there was something else. "You're suddenly really okay with this."

"I need to finish everything in Wonderland, right? It's going to keep coming for me if I don't finish. I suppose I could start saying no, but I can't seem to find the person who is in charge any longer. Not that I could before. The Queen of Hearts may control the castle, but Wonderland itself is a terrible listener and is very opposed to taking my requests. Actually, the Queen of Hearts is also bad about that. How do I send these?"

Adrianna couldn't help but smile at that. They might be the same age, but Alice just did not do well with technology.

It was worse than her dad asking Lance to show him how to do anything with his computer. Maybe when she wasn't so entranced in Wonderland she could...

Out of the corner of her eye, Adrianna saw a flash of something and looked at the mirror. At first she thought it might have been Arthur, but it was from the other side of the mirror. It was lines and lines of people of all sizes, most of them not even human. They stood in lines, holding spears and swords, staring blankly ahead. "Alice..."

Alice followed her line of sight and saw Wonderland looking back from the mirror. All at once, the mirror was a mirror again.

"Sorry."

"That's been happening a lot lately," Adrianna said. Alice should know if she didn't already.

"Has it?"

Adrianna nodded. "Can anything get out?"

"Besides Cat, I don't know."

"It's okay," she said. "You can show me how to get the hearts back in place and I'll finish it up for you. And then you can leave Wonderland behind, right? Start focusing more on here."

Alice nodded and went back to her bed with a book. Even with all the world at her fingers between her phone and the computer, she still went back to books. At some point,

Adrianna would get Lance to teach her to use the internet better. Maybe if they spent more time together, Lance could finally tell Alice how he felt about her. It might even go well.

For now, Adrianna went to her phone and saw Alice's email. At least she knew how to attach a file. Her files were a lot better than going through the book that felt so unsettling under her fingers and Adrianna abandoned it in front of her on the bed to try and pick out one of these to try first.

There was a thrill to it that she hadn't expected. If she could really do this, it was *magic*. She might actually be able to do *magic*. As a child she had imagined she had a magic wand that could make anything she dreamed of happen and she was so close to being able to do it. She could be the princess she once dreamed of. That she still, in quiet moments when she was all alone, dreamed of.

Or, at the very least, she could use it to make her bag a little lighter. Even now, she could feel a knot forming in her shoulder from how heavy her backpack was.

"*Ábedecian gliwere snytrian eormencynn hércyme.*"

It was supposed to summon her brothers. Alice had a specific note that it was supposed to summon any of the Case triplets, so Adrianna watched the door expectantly, hoping that it worked. She thought she felt something when she said the words, but that may have just been her desire for it to work and for her childhood dreams to come true. Her older brain was caught on something else.

"I think the sentence structure's off," Adrianna said. "It's just verb, noun, adjective. Is that how it's supposed to be?"

"It's what worked," Alice said. "I figured that's all there was to it."

Adrianna went quiet, eyes still on the door. After a long moment of nothing, she shifted and asked, "How do you know if..."

"You don't know if it's working until they show up," Alice told her.

They sat in silence, Alice going back to her novel. Adrianna kept staring at the door, trying to tell herself that it worked. It worked for Alice, so it might work for her too. She could help Alice if she could get this working.

Even with her eyes glued on the door and hoping for it to happen, Adrianna still jumped when there was a knock at the door. She leaped up and darted over to open it, finding Adam there and looking confused. He took only a moment to recover before he came up with a reason to be there.

"Have you talked to Lance lately?" he asked. "Something's weird."

Adrianna got up and looked down the hall. "No, but he might be here in a minute," she said. "Come in."

Adam stopped just inside the door, staring at the book

open on her bed. "What the hell is going on here?" he demanded, looking at Alice. "I thought you said those things were dangerous."

"Wonderland is much too impatient to wait for me," Alice told him, putting down her book. "Very inconsiderate. And if you keep talking like that, I may just have to leave *you* to ensure Adrianna doesn't go mad."

"You shouldn't be reading those," Adam told Adrianna. "It's not your job to do it. It's *hers*. She can't just abandon Wonderland like she keeps trying to."

"One day I'll figure out just what it is they did for you," Alice mused. "Perhaps if I ask nicely enough, Wonderland will let you take my place and stand in my shoes. They are not very large shoes to fill, though. I think you'll be quite uncomfortable in them."

"Do you have to do that?"

Adam let himself in, looking annoyed as he kicked the door closed before he sat down on Adrianna's bed. He started flipping through the brown book and moving it away from Adrianna as she tried to snatch it away from him. "What are these things anyway? Lily never let me touch the red one. Said it was cursed."

"Magic books," Alice told him. "They don't belong in Wonderland any more than you do."

"And you do?"

"Like a foot in a very tattered sock," she said. "Or that was how it was when I left before. I don't think they quite fixed the hole yet. She might know, though."

Alice smiled at the mirror and drew Adam and Adrianna's attention there. Tiger Lily looked confused as she stared out and Alice appeared in front of it, taking a seat and smiling. "Hello. I wasn't expecting to see you here. You should have knocked. Not very polite to just stand there, not looking."

"Hello, Alice of Wonderland," Tiger Lily said, coming closer to her side of the mirror. "You are still unwell."

"Just a headache," Alice insisted. She looked back to Adam's accusing glare as he got closer. "I think I've been opening mirrors."

"A lot," Adrianna said.

"Sorry. But!" She turned back to Tiger Lily. "What happened?" she asked. "I needed to go back. What happened out there? Have you had any luck with the castle?"

Adam went to the mirror and tried to touch it, but his hand hit the glass. "You could just take us through so we could see for ourselves," he told her, annoyance rising in his voice.

"You are better with your family," Tiger Lily told him. "It is safe there."

"Still drawn back, are you?" came another silky voice, the Cheshire Cat appearing around Tiger Lily's shoulders. Tiger Lily grabbed him and threw him off, though he was soon sliding back next to her, watching Alice as Alice watched him and smiling. "Would you like to return for a cup of tea?" he asked, watching her carefully. "I think your manners might be better now."

"I'd just like to know what happened," Alice told him. "Have you managed to move the castle out of Neverland at all?"

"*What* happened?" Adam demanded.

"Of course not," Cat said. "A castle with such a stubborn Queen will not take requests. It still tries to flee Wonderland, though now there are people watching it again. Ones who don't believe in tea time, the savages."

Tiger Lily looked like she might try to take his ear, but Cat moved along her shoulders as if her head were nothing more than an inconsiderate vase on a shelf that really would do better on the floor. "The hole in the world remains, still leaking out terrible nightmares with terrible manners."

"Neverland is full of zombies," Alice said by way of explanation. "They were coming across. Arthur wanted to fight the castle."

"He disappeared with it."

"I brought them back here, actually."

"Good," Tiger Lily said. "I do not trust that Arthur. He smells strange. And your brother as well," she added, looking at Adam. "There is something wrong with him."

"You're telling me," Adam muttered, standing behind Alice and frowning.

Adrianna stared at the door. "Shouldn't Lance be here by now too?"

"Why would he be?" Adam asked.

"I summoned both of you. Only you showed up. The only difference was the name, so it should have been the same for both of them, right?" She looked to Alice, curious and uncertain.

She thought about it. "When is a door not a door?" Alice asked.

"What are you talking about?"

"Maybe it's not working because you're not calling him properly." She paused, looking at Adam. "You know, I wonder if that's why it didn't work with you. I'd call, but you never came, no matter how hard I tried. You must have been a different Adam while you were there."

"He may not have shown himself, but he was there," came the silky melodious tones of the Cheshire Cat. He appeared at the mirror next to Tiger Lily and passed across, turning into the tall boy with the purple hair as he came across. He slunk over to Adam, taller than him now and smiling too wide for his face. "Hiding so he wouldn't have to go home."

"Tell me you didn't," Adrianna pleaded. Alice had spent so long looking for him, so many weekends. She'd come back in such a state sometimes. And he'd been there the whole time whenever she called.

"He did," Tiger Lily confirmed. "He would stop and he would leave. But he would shrink so he would not be found."

"Rude," Alice said. "But it doesn't really explain why Lance isn't here."

"Because, Alice dear, he is not a door." The Cheshire Cat smiled wide. "That much you were very right about." He faded away bit by bit, going off somewhere in the school to cause trouble while Alice looked back into the mirror. She shrugged and closed it with a wave to Tiger Lily. Alice wasn't nearly as bothered by the revelation as Adrianna was.

Adam looked down at her and grinned. "If you don't need me, I'm going," he said, heading for the door. "Don't let my sister get too into those magic books, Alice. You know how dangerous they are."

Adrianna watched him go, a smile spreading across her face. She had done it. *Magic.* She had done magic, and Adam's bad mood wouldn't take that away from her.

CHAPTER 17

All New Alice

THE HEADACHE WOULDN'T go away. No matter what painkillers Alice took, the dull throbbing in the back of her head pounded through her thoughts over and over again until she barely noticed it anymore. It was a problem that she rectified by trying not to talk too much.

Unfortunately, Sarah had invited her out with them after Combat Club and Alice said yes. It seemed like a nice enough thing to do. She wasn't ready to go back to Wonderland just yet and she was happy to have something else to distract herself. She had barely spent any time with them since getting back, worried about what Heather might remember. Despite turning into a raccoon, she showed no signs of even remembering the incident.

It was surprising when Heather agreed that Alice should come back to Combat Club, that she could try not disappearing for a weekend for once. They met in the morning to head down to the town, to the street filled with small shops and went immediately to a small coffee shop where everyone behind the counter knew Sarah's order.

"You're actually around this weekend?" Kevin asked, surprised.

"Where's Rob?" Sarah asked, looking around for the group of them. Her eyes fell on Heather as she added, "And Adam, for that matter."

"Adam's seeing a doctor about those scratches," Heather said. "Getting shots or something maybe? He didn't really say."

"Rob's got a meeting with a guy who wants to give him money," Kevin said dismissively before turning back on Heather. "I'm more surprised you're here. You've been as much of a ghost on the weekends as Alice."

Heather smiled. "Just lucky this time," she said. "Last weekend was *everything*. I don't even remember half of it. And I haven't spent any time with you guys."

"Aw, we're on your checklist," Kevin teased.

Heather shoved him back, laughing and settling in as they started to roam the streets. "You're lucky I don't abandon you guys to study," she said. "I swear, Mr. Oak hates me."

"I heard he's an asshole to everyone in the scholarship program," Sarah said. "Don't take it personally. He just doesn't want you here."

"Thanks." Heather rolled her eyes. "It's fine. It's Math. If I get the answer right, he can't even knock my grade down. And if he does, he'll never hear the end of it."

"Making enemies in the faculty," Kevin said, sounding almost proud.

Alice stayed quiet as they chattered. Adrianna said she needed to catch up, but she was pretty sure she should have known Heather was on a scholarship well before this. And that Sarah had been to this store before, given the way the staff greeted her like an old friend. It had been far too long and she had not been paying any attention.

"Actually, since I have both of you here," Heather said suddenly as she turned back to Sarah and looked back at Alice. She paused, trying to think about her words before she let them out. "Any idea why everyone hates Nike all of a sudden? I mean, after Wyatt decked him last year..."

"None of it's true, but he deserves everything he's getting," Sarah said, her voice cold and sharp.

"But what *happened?*" Heather pressed. "Both of you guys went out with him. I mean, he dumped both of you, but—"

Kevin laughed. "Didn't I tell you about how I broke them up?" he asked. "I told you I didn't like him. He got mad because I just talked to Alice. Thought she was cheating and dumped her right there."

"He kept giving me things like it would make me like him more," Alice remembered. "If he wanted me to return in kind, he probably should have attempted to be a completely different person, though I doubt that would fit very well in a box. Or that I would have liked that much either."

Alice frowned, her mind going back to the emails that Lori had been sending. The one on asexuality haunted her and she didn't much like how thinking about it now was making her feel.

She felt Adrianna's look of concern. "The only reason you went out with him at all was because of me," she said. "Wyatt needed someone to go out with his roommate."

"You never liked him," Kevin said. "You could have said no."

"Oh, Lance threatened me," she said, smiling and pushing the email out of her mind.

"Speaking of," Sarah said, looking across the street. "You remember back when there were three of them?"

Adrianna's face scrunched and she blinked. She was bothered by something. "We still don't know where he is," Adrianna said. "After this long, they say we shouldn't hold out much hope for Matt to come back, but…"

"But Adam showed up fine," Kevin said. "And never said where he went."

"All three of them went missing at the same time, but it

took two years for Adam to come back," Heather noted. "And he still won't tell me where he was. But someone knows."

Alice smiled as she watched Lance and Arthur come across the street. "I'm sure he'll tell you one day," she said. "You'll just have to ask the right questions. And you tend to get mad whenever someone gives you the answers you're asking for, so perhaps it's better not to ask at all."

A snicker came out of Sarah, but that flicker of concern crossed back over Adrianna's face. Heather glowered at her for only a moment before she relaxed again. "Heads up, we're going to have company," she said, nodding to the door.

Arthur made his way in with Lance, both laughing about something and heading over to join them. Arthur looked perfectly pleased with himself, his eyes on Adrianna and making no effort to hide that. Alice wasn't bothered, happy to not have to deal with him for a bit, but there was something else a little concerning.

Lance looked pale and winded from just walking and a little laughter. Adrianna seemed to notice as well, watching her brother carefully and ignoring the one handed boy that put his prosthetic hand on the back of her chair and leaned over her.

"You feeling okay?" Adrianna asked.

Lance's face scrunched up at the question. "I'm good," he said, offended that she would ask. He looked very quickly away from her to Alice, flashing a smile that she had never seen on him before. She frowned at it, not sure what he was trying to do.

"Funny seeing you here," Arthur said to Adrianna, ignoring the other people around them. "We were thinking about heading down to the theatre and catching a movie if you wanted to join us."

"What movie?" Heather asked. She was the only one interested, though Sarah was keeping a careful eye on them.

"We'll find out when we get there," Arthur told her. "Well?"

"I'm all right, thanks," Adrianna said, knowing he was looking at her. The smile on her face was hollow, as she got up and grabbed her purse. "You guys go ahead, I need to pick up a few things. Alice, are you coming?"

"Yeah," Alice said, following Adrianna out away from the place and down the street.

They said nothing for a block, Alice simply staying in step beside her and following until Adrianna came to a stop at the store window. "I don't like him," she said finally, frowning at the window. "It feels weird when he stares at me, and he keeps doing it. Who is he?"

Alice shrugged. "Arthur Pendragon. Penn now, I suppose. A name means quite a bit, so perhaps he had lost his dragon along with his hand. I hope he won't go chasing a dragon. Although, perhaps he will to impress you. Though you have already proven to be just fine at befriending dragons on your own."

Adrianna paused for a long moment before she turned back to Alice, concern still on her face now etched deeply into it. "Do you know you're doing that?" she asked.

"I'm doing... Oh."

"You sound like you're from Wonderland," Adrianna explained. "Since you disappeared the last time, you've been talking a little funny. Since you got that headache that won't go away."

"There are neurological issues that result in headaches and strange speech patterns," Alice said. She didn't really want to talk about why she knew that, or that she might have the medication for that particular combination of symptoms somewhere, long expired though it may be.

"You know that's not it," Adrianna said, leading her into the store. "Wonderland's getting to you. The longer you deal with it, the more it's affecting you. You need to finish whatever it is it wants you to do so it will let you go."

Alice nodded dumbly as she followed her in. "I haven't been talking much," Alice said. "Maybe no one's noticed."

"That's not really the point," Adrianna said gently. She reached back like she was going to take Alice's hand, but thought better of it. "It's taking you over. It's probably bad for you."

"Nothing is bad on purpose," Alice said, looking at one of the trinkets on the shelves. "Nothing really intends to be terrible. It is just by unfortunate accident that it intends to be. Except in cases of rudeness, where it is absolutely intentional."

"Alice..."

Alice smiled and bit back what her mouth wanted to say. "Shutting up."

A deep, beleaguered sigh escaped her. "We need to get your business done in Wonderland," she said. "That's how you get it to leave you alone."

Alice nodded but said nothing. Her head was throbbing, but she continued to follow Adrianna around the shop and into the next one. She didn't see what was so bad about it. Sure, there was the headache but Heather was talking to her again. Everyone else seemed to be fine with her. It wasn't really much worse than it had been before. Surely no one but Adrianna had noticed what she was saying.

She wondered if it was the hole in Wonderland that was doing it. That was probably it. She imagined Peter was probably dealing with the same issue. Or he would have been if...

Well, maybe Matt was dealing with it.

Still, Wonderland had left her alone for years already and there wasn't much that had changed. She had lost friends and been caged then. She was going to go back to her father and into imprisonment again once the school year was done. He wouldn't let her see anyone during the holiday. It was like being thrown into an asylum. She wasn't sure Wonderland calling her back was really so bad. If she actually went during the holidays, it would be a welcome escape.

If she refused to go again, would it stop calling her? If it stopped calling her, would she lose the ability to go on her own? She wasn't sure she wanted that. Would she stop being like a treacle? It seemed so strange that she wouldn't be able to do that anymore. That she would have to give it all up. That she'd have to say goodbye to even Cat. That was something she didn't know she wanted to do. Even Cat...

"Hey."

Alice jumped as Kevin appeared next to her. She'd lost Adrianna at some point and she looked around now, trying to figure out where she was. At Kevin's look, she stopped and decided she was just where she needed to be for right now. Here was where she was and here was a perfectly fine place.

"Where's Addie?" he asked.

"She's right where she is," Alice said. "Shopping, I suppose. That's what she was doing when I saw her last, anyway."

"Makes sense," Kevin said, though he didn't look like he quite believed her. "Look, I wanted to ask you something a little weird. Have you talked to Peter at all?"

Alice shook her head. "I saw him at Combat Club this morning."

"Do you know what's going on with him? He's been a bit weird lately. Since… Heather told me you guys both collapsed, right? And I think it's been since about then." There was something else he wasn't saying. That she'd been weird too. She wondered how many other people had noticed. When it wasn't Adrianna, she felt a little thrill of panic, that her father might find out and take her away. She needed to try to be normal.

"It's fine," she said. "We got up and it was all good."

"He's gotten happier," he blurted out. "Like, he's sleep—sleep*walking* but he's just happier for some reason and I'm worried he's not telling me everything. I know you know something. About where he's really from. You know something." He stared at her and Alice wondered if that was why he was looking at her strangely. He was straighter, staring her in the eye and holding himself firm though he was starting to flush. Embarrassed by the comment and worried he was wrong.

She knew she shouldn't admit that she knew anything, but Kevin was so sure. There was only one polite route to go. "There are many things I know and many more that I don't know about Peter Pan," she said. "The only ones who really know where he came from, I imagine, are him and his mother."

Kevin's eyes went wide and looked past her to the window. He wasn't even paying attention to what she was saying, staring and caught between fascination and fear.

She looked back and saw the cards parading back and forth outside the castle grounds. A man made of many parts left the castle, a child under his arm not moving with a hole in his chest. In the air, the thin crack of darkness in the distance where Wonderland and Neverland were starting to blend together grew thicker.

Alice's eyes flew wide and she shut the portal down, returning it to just a window reflecting the world behind them. She looked back at Kevin and he took a step back, his hands starting to rise in front of him.

"Nothing," he said firmly. "I saw absolutely nothing."

Alice's jaw set. Maybe Adrianna was right. She was going to get sent away if weird stuff kept happening around her, and that was worse than being surrounded by Wonderland and being called back there to do their bidding all the time.

Maybe she should go back and see what it wanted.

She let out a breath, looking at Kevin. He looked so startled, but still so determined. Like he really wasn't going to say anything. Like he was too scared to say a word.

"He's okay, though," Alice said. "He gave it away. He said he's going to grow up now."

Kevin relaxed, though he kept looking at the window. He started walking just a little too quickly, ushering Alice away from there as well. "He wasn't lying, then," he said. "Let's find Addie. She can't have gotten far, right?"

CHAPTER **18**

Familiar

BEAN MIGHT HAVE only mediocre coffee, but their honey lemon tea was amazing for Adrianna after choir. Song after song was still going through her mind, silently trying to hit the lower notes she was struggling with. There were always a few who said she could go into this professionally, but after everything Joe had told her, she never wanted to pursue music as a career. It was a hard life and she thought something more academic might suit her better. Her grades were doing so much better this year already. The homework was only difficult in volume, and she had figured out how to manage that.

What she hadn't learned to manage was the strangeness of her roommate. She was sure Alice's constant headache was getting worse, but she wouldn't go to the nurse about it. There were glimpses of Wonderland in the reflections more and more often. For how much Alice tried to stay quiet, when she did speak there was that tinge of something off about everything she said that permeated her words more often than not. Something, Adrianna knew, had changed about Wonderland and it was doing something to Alice.

Alice wouldn't tell her more about what happened when she was there, so she found the only other person who might know. Peter was rarely not surrounded by friends, but she caught him in the large study room of the middle school dorms anyway and asked for just a moment of his time outside. He frowned, but joined her out in the late November afternoon.

"Did something happen?" he asked. "I'm not doing any of this stuff anymore, Addie. I'm done."

"Nothing happened," she assured him. "I just want to know how it went in Wonderland last time. Alice has been different. I'm worried."

"Oh. She didn't tell you? Someone rammed a castle into the wall between Neverland and Wonderland. Ripped a huge hole in it."

Adrianna knew that was bad, but she didn't know how that caused a headache that never stopped. "Was there anything else?" she asked.

"Yeah, I gave away Neverland," he said. "Now I don't

have to deal with it anymore. I told Alice she should do it too, but I don't think she has yet."

"What... You can just give it away?" The possibilities circled her mind. It could be so easy for her to leave it all behind. All she needed to do was find someone else to take the world from her and she could be free to actually enjoy herself.

But Alice wouldn't make someone else deal with it for her. She wouldn't want to bother someone else with that kind of burden. And it was a burden, whether Alice could see the ways it weighed on her or not. She knew Adam would gladly take it off her hands, but Adrianna didn't want to see her brother suffering like Alice was either.

"I figured out how," Peter said. "Alice acts like she's so smart. She can do it too. Otherwise she's gonna have to save it and I don't know how she's gonna do that anymore. There's a lot of people with hearts to put back and Tiger Lily said she can't do it anymore."

"Because she's been cursed. But there are ways to fix that."

Adrianna jumped as Arthur and Lance joined them. She was getting used to Arthur lingering in the corner of her eye again. He'd gone back to watching her from afar again and she was getting very accustomed to ignoring him so long as he didn't try to do anything to talk to her. Having him and Lance just walk up to them was startling.

"We don't need your help, Arthur," Adrianna said firmly.

"Have you asked your brother what he did to me yet?" he asked. "You should feel lucky I'm still willing to help you at all."

"Which one?"

"Maybe you should ask what he's doing to that brother," Peter said, pointing at Lance. "What the hell happened to you?"

He had a point. Lance was pale, even for him, and the smile on his face didn't quite reach his dead eyes. His face didn't even look like his own, but like someone else had taken over the duties of his expressions for him. The dark shadows under his eyes weren't unusual when he was in the middle of a project, but it certainly didn't help. Stranger, he had the slightest hint of a shadow forming under his cheeks, making him look sick.

Still, he smiled and hooked an arm around Peter's shoulders like Matt might have done once and tugged him away. "You worry like an old lady," he said, the grin on his face still looking off. "Come on, let the lovebirds have their dance."

"You smell weird," Peter said as he was dragged away. He glanced back at Adrianna, concern across his face, but Adrianna nodded for him to go. It would be okay. She had things she needed to say to Arthur as it was, and this seemed like as good an opportunity as any.

Adrianna took in a deep breath, trying to brace herself for this, and turned back to Arthur. "I don't want you to keep following me around," she told him. Directly should work, right? He would listen to her if he liked her so much. She was getting better at not paying attention when he was there, but it had been better when he took a break. Whatever had caught his attention then, she hoped he would go back to that.

Arthur looked at her and those eyes made her heart thump a little heavier. He was being creepy, she reminded herself. He was following her around everywhere she went just because he thought she was pretty and that wasn't right. It wasn't flattering. It was creepy.

"I was only walking by," he told her. "Nothing wrong with that."

"I mean, while I'm in class. If you're not in the class, you shouldn't be there. You have your own classes."

"They're much less interesting than you are."

Adrianna stepped back before he could touch her, but he didn't make a move. "I don't want you watching me anymore," she repeated. "Stop."

Arthur put his hands up. "If the beauty wishes for me to stop admiring her, who am I to refuse?" he asked. "But that's not why I stopped today. You were wondering what to do about Alice. You don't seem to realize she's been cursed and that you have someone who can break that curse on her right here."

"You don't know she's cursed."

"She stopped being able to return hearts one day, wasn't it?" he asked. "You don't just lose a skill like that on your own. Someone has to do something to take that from you."

"She can put them back again."

"Can she?"

Adrianna wanted to say yes, to make him stop and leave her alone, but she couldn't. Alice thought she could, but she had said it was hard. That Tiger Lily had stopped her from doing more. That it still was so hard to do. Alice might think she could, but it was clear that she was still having trouble.

Arthur kept staring at her and it was hard to breathe. Her heart was beating hard in her chest. She couldn't let him have this. She wouldn't say yes to him, not even if he made her feel this way.

"Even if she is, what are you going to do about it?"

"I'll cure her of that curse the same way I cured you of yours," he said. "A fairy gave me the gift of a kiss that can break any curse. It would be a shame if I didn't use it to help you. For a price, of course."

"Price?"

"One date."

She stared at him. She wouldn't agree to this. She wouldn't let herself spend too long alone with him. "No."

Arthur smiled and straightened up. Adrianna didn't even realize how close he had gotten until he waved for Lance to come back and join him. "You will be mine," Arthur promised her. "Either with kindness, or another way." His eyes went meaningfully to Lance as he and Peter came back to join them. Adrianna felt her stomach drop as, without another word to her, the pair of them walked away.

Her heart was still beating heavy in her chest, her nose filled with the scent of the forest. She didn't like that he made her feel this way. He was a creep and she shouldn't feel this way. But even so, she watched him as he left. Once she realized she was doing it, she forced her gaze to Lance, though Arthur stayed close by in her mind.

"You said Lance smelled weird," she said at the concerned look on Peter's face.

"Your whole family smells funny."

Adrianna wasn't sure if that should offend her. "But what about Lance?"

"Smells like he's missing something," Peter said. "Kind of like people in Neverland after Wendy…."

Adrianna let him trail off, not sure what that meant. From what she had heard about Wendy, she was almost certain she didn't want him to finish what he was saying. "What about Arthur?"

"Like fairy," Peter said. He looked sad and he turned away to leave. "I've got homework."

Adrianna watched him go as well, not sure what else to do. She needed to talk to someone. Maybe Alice would know what to do. She had dealt with this sort of thing before, right? And she had found Arthur.

Or, she thought as she kept walking, she didn't have to bother her with it at all. Alice had sent her notes from the books. She could do magic. If Alice was there, she could practice and learn more, maybe figure out a way to fix it for herself. But she felt guilty about troubling Alice with this. She had more than enough to deal with on her own without having to figure out how to make Arthur leave her alone and stop threatening her family.

Adrianna got back to their room and found Alice there, but she had fallen asleep on the bed. Instead of a novel, her computer was open on a forum tinged in purple accents that didn't look like it was for any classes. She closed it and moved it to the desk for her so Alice didn't roll over on it before lying down on her own bed to scroll through her phone, looking through Alice's notes.

Slowly, Adrianna formed a plan. If she practiced, she could get good with magic. And if she spent enough time with the books, surely she could figure out how to break any curse that might be on Alice. If there was a curse at all and that wasn't something Arthur was just saying to make her go out with him. If there wasn't a curse, she would get good enough to help Alice wrap up everything in Wonderland so that the world would leave her alone.

She could even use that magic to figure out how to help Lance and get him away from whatever Arthur was doing to him. And Arthur was definitely doing something to him. He looked so unwell and he wasn't acting at all like himself. She should have talked to him before now, should have known something was wrong. She needed to find a way to help him too.

She just had to learn magic. And with that magic she could...

Thoughts of what she would actually have to do started as she hit one part of Alice's documents. How to put back a heart. She could think about it fine if Alice was doing it. Somehow, she never really thought about what it involved when she did. But this, the description of having to adjust so that the aortas lined up properly, she realized that this meant she would have to be around actual real hearts. That she would touch them...

She shuddered at the thought.

Next to her, Alice stirred and got out of bed. Adrianna perked up, hoping that she could help her figure out how to actually do some of these spells. She opened her mouth to say something, but closed it quickly.

Her eyes were closed. Alice was still asleep.

"Alice?" Adrianna asked. She got to her feet to stop her. You weren't supposed to wake up a sleepwalker, right? But Alice was already wandering into a wall. She should stop her from hurting herself. "Hey Alice, you're going to—"

Alice vanished before she hit the wall and reappeared on the other side of the room. The mirror on the wardrobe had become the interior of a castle and Alice walked through before Adrianna could do anything to stop her.

CHAPTER 19

Direction

ALICE SAT AT the side of the classroom by the window, just like she did every History class, but this was not History. She had a book in front of her, devoid of words, and a pen in her hands that refused to write. There were no other students in the room, though Alice could still hear their chatter around her. There was no teacher at the front of the room, only the logo for AVEN written on the board with the inverted triangle and an explanation of asexuality written on a purple chalkboard. Everything in here was tinged in purple, like the sunrise had chosen something other than fire to paint the room with.

Outside was nothing but grayscale madness. Trees reached up into the sky to snatch flying children to devour. Crawling out from under the roots were foxes holding their own hearts wandering off in search of a sword. Flowers grew and scolded anyone who came too near for blocking the sun. In the sky, day and night fought in a white and black patchwork, burning into spirals that would occasionally rain down bright red hearts onto the land below.

Alice didn't know where she would rather be. She was supposed to be in class, supposed to be taking notes, but there were no other people here. She could hear them, and when she wasn't looking she thought they might be there. But her eyes wouldn't catch any of them. There wasn't even a teacher at the front of the class, and she didn't want to learn anymore.

It didn't matter if the word was right or wrong. She wasn't going to tell anyone if it was true. She was already different enough. She didn't need another reason.

But she needed to stay in class. Class was where she belonged.

Out in the monochrome, she could now see people trying to get her attention. They were in trouble without her. The foxes were throwing hearts at them, burying them under the beating organs. More fell from the sky.

But she needed to stay in class.

She couldn't figure out which friends were there or how many, only that they needed her. They were going to die without her. She had to go out there.

But she needed to…

A woman appeared at the front of the room, looking

around like she was displeased with everything she was see-ing. Alice knew this woman. Adrianna's stepmother, who was now dressed like she was out of a fantasy novel. The woman who said her name was Morgana now. She was the teacher, and Alice had something else to focus on than her peers' chat-ter or her friends dying out the window.

"Follow me," Morgana said. "I want to talk. And when we are done, I have something for you."

Alice did as she was asked. When Morgana vanished and appeared further down the hall, Alice did too. When the school stopped being a school and turned into nothing at all, Alice welcomed it and continued to follow.

Morgana vanished again and kept walking further into the nothing, but Alice couldn't follow this time. Something had grabbed her, was stopping her. Something had her arm and was pulling it back and wouldn't let go. Something was hissing in her ear, telling her to go somewhere else. Some-thing was asking her to open her eyes. Something struck her hard across the face.

HER CHEEK STUNG as she stumbled back but Alice couldn't fall too far. Someone had her arms and kept her up, was pulling her along. Pressed between Alice and the per-son forcing her forward was a very warm, still moving bag of things that kept slipping and being pulled back up as it sandwiched between them.

Hearts. Alice knew right away that thing pressed into her back was a bag full of hearts.

"Alice of Wonderland you must wake up," Tiger Lily hissed in her ear, pushing her forward on stumbling feet. Alice struggled to keep up the pace. "This is not the time to be asleep!"

"Only resting my eyes," Alice assured her, looking around as they nearly tumbled over. Tiger Lily let her go as soon as she spoke, letting Alice gather her feet under her. She looked around for the first time and saw very quickly why Tiger Lily was so determined to keep moving.

Around her was a very familiar castle, decorated in garish red. The Queen of Hearts had very little subtlety in terms of home decor and Alice would be happy to help her find literally any other colour to add to her colour palette, but that was not what Tiger Lily seemed more worried about right now. She was much more worried about the people following them in a quick march, weaponry at the ready.

"Yes, I do think it's time to go," Alice said.

"I will meet you outside," Tiger Lily assured her, popping something into her mouth. She shoved the bag of hearts into Alice's hands. "Await me by the tree. The one where the Jabberwocky sleeps."

Tiger Lily didn't so much vanish as she got very small very quickly. Alice looked from the spot she had vanished and back to the fast approaching contingent, then to the bag of hearts she now held in her hands. With a sigh, she took a step away and went outside the castle to try and find this tree with the Jabberwocky in it.

IT SEEMED SILLY to even look. The Jabberwocky had always preferred caves to trees, so there was no reason for a tree to be a better home. Dragons tended to breathe fire, and had a rather poor relationship with things that could be kindling. Back when the Jabberwocky had been in the woods outside the school, he had hidden away in a cave that he had melted into glass. A tree was no home for a dragon.

Still, Alice looked. Tiger Lily had become very small, she hoped this meeting place was not too far or she would be waiting for a very long time for her to appear. She didn't stray far from the castle, wandering about outside of the walls and looking back and forth for something. There were people here now, people from Wonderland who had very clearly lost their hearts. Alice wondered if she should be helping with that. If any of the hearts in this bag of hers belonged to any of them.

If she even could...

She kept looking for this impossible tree that was so much

better than a cave when she spotted it. There was a large willow, one that looked like it had been grown specifically to be a pillow for a very large creature, sitting shortly past where day cracked open and turned into a horrific night. Curled up atop of it was a dragon with its snout on sideways, fast asleep and paying no attention to any of the madness happening around him. The strangeness stayed well away from the willow as well, like it knew full well that there was a dragon that might set them and itself on fire if it were disturbed.

And she was going to risk disturbing it by going close. With a sigh, Alice went closer, taking her time. Tiger Lily was very small, so she would be a while. The Jabberwocky didn't stir from Alice coming closer, or from what she was sure were very loud thoughts about whether she was going to have to bend down to see Tiger Lily. It felt like that might be rude. And Tiger Lily hadn't done such a thing. But she had been barely as tall as Alice's ankle. This would be a very awkward conversation indeed.

"Pardon me," Alice said, keeping her voice low enough that the Jabberwocky would not stir. He seemed out cold, but she didn't really trust him to stay that way. Still, she dropped the bag of hearts next to the trunk and took a seat herself.

She should try to return the hearts. Try to return one. She could do it again. She could do the spell if...

Even thinking about the spell she needed made her dizzy.

She was glad she was already sitting, but that only meant that she was lower to the ground where the sadness wanted her. She had done it before, had pushed through it. One had gone back. Was it only a fluke? Was she really not better at all?

The hearts were still thrumming next to her without a care in the world. They didn't mind that they weren't where they were meant to be. Alice wished she could feel the same, but she did not. She felt like she was meant to be returning... returning... to the castle. She had a very important meeting at the castle.

Alice rose to her feet, leaving the hearts behind her. Tiger Lily could find them well enough. And the Jabberwocky would guard them from anything that might try to take them. And she was probably still within the bounds of fashionably late for a meeting if she hurried.

"Where are you going, Alice of Wonderland?"

Alice didn't look back and didn't stop walking. Tiger Lily didn't sound very small anymore. "You sound taller," she said. "You should be able to carry that bag of hearts yourself now."

"Where are you going, Alice of Wonderland?" she asked again, sounding tired.

"I have a meeting at the castle," she said. "I mustn't keep them waiting long. I feel I can still be fashionably late if I leave now."

"A meeting with who?" Tiger Lily was moving now and

Alice was soon looking at her. She grabbed Alice by the shoulders and stopped her, peering into her eyes. "You look like Adam whenever he spoke of his missing brother."

"I'm fine."

Tiger Lily looked like she was going to say something, but held herself back. "Come," she said, taking Alice by the hand and leading her away. "Tell me who you were going to meet."

Alice thought about it and frowned. "I don't know."

"We will talk to the Caterpillar," she said, pulling Alice along. "Things are changing, Alice of Wonderland. It may not be safe for you here any longer."

CHAPTER 20

Banished

THE FOREST WAS welcome, though she still felt like she should be somewhere else. The castle. She should be there. But Tiger Lily needed her to talk to someone else first. And Alice still didn't know who she was going to see in the castle or what they were meeting about. It was awfully rude of her to come unprepared, and more rude of whoever invited her to not send a formal invitation.

Tiger Lily would not let go of her hand, though they were in no hurry as they went onward. Alice was aware that she had things she should be doing right now. If it was the morning, she should go to Combat Club. If she had missed that, she still had to meet Adrianna for lunch. And after that, there was still Library for her in the afternoon for an hour. She might have said she would go out with people on Sunday as well. She really shouldn't be here all weekend.

She was only supposed to be here for a meeting. Hopefully a quick one. And that had already gone awry.

She was led to a familiar table with broken cups and broken clocks littered across the ground. No one appeared to be there, the tea party long since over and the guests gone home, but Tiger Lily brought her to the far side of the table. There was a deep fog lingering around it, a smoke that smelled of apples.

Alice felt her mind clear as she breathed in. She hoped they weren't going to try to give her a pie or something, but she could see no food on the table. Whatever this meeting was for, they hadn't done anything that they should in order to ensure their guests were content. She had to wonder if this was because they were coming unannounced, as Tiger Lily didn't seem to have a plan as she dragged Alice down to the ground without so much as laying down a cushion first.

"Caterpillar, she has returned," she said. Tiger Lily folded her feet under her and finally let Alice go. "I found her in the castle."

"Not a very polite greeting," the Caterpillar told her. He took in another deep drag of his hookah and breathed it out, looking around until he laid his eyes on Alice. He watched her, waiting.

"Hello," Alice said, inclining her head. She was already

sitting, which made a curtsy very difficult. "I do hope we are not disturbing you."

"Of course you are disturbing me," he said. "But it is a disruption that must be made. Wonderland is in a great deal of trouble and you have not been here enough, Alice. You have a duty and you have been carelessly shirking it for silly, frivolous things. And now that we need you to shy away, you have decided that you must appear again. You must learn when you are wanted."

"If I weren't meant to be here, then I'm sure I wouldn't be able to be here," Alice said, not sure what she was supposed to take from this. They didn't want her here? Didn't she still have to put the hearts back? Not that she could do it the same as she could before...

"You have your own key and you use another's door nonetheless." He took another long drag, thinking it over for far too long before he exhaled again, this time the smoke coming out in shades of pink and purple. "Don't get me so off topic, Alice. It's quite hard enough to concentrate without your nonsense."

An irritated noise escaped Alice and she saw a smile flicker across Tiger Lily's lips. Alice stayed quiet, folding her hands in front of her and tightening her jaw so she could not say anything else.

"Alice doesn't know about the woman yet," Tiger Lily

said. She looked back at Alice. "There is a woman in the castle. We think that she is responsible for the castle moving."

"Claudia?" Alice asked. She could kind of remember that
she was there now, though she wasn't sure why she would be.
She wasn't with the Cases any longer, Adrianna had mentioned that much, but her being in Wonderland felt strange.
"Or did I dream that?"

"Morgana," Caterpillar told her.

"Yes. That's what she said to call her now." She looked
between the two of their curious expressions. "She's Adrianna's stepmother."

"Your friend has poor taste in stepmothers," Tiger Lily
said. She looked down at something in her pocket.

"Do you know what a stepmother is?"

"No."

"Enough silliness," Caterpillar snapped back at them.
"Alice cannot return to Wonderland again. It is much too
dangerous for Wonderland. And I quite like Wonderland.
Much more than I like Alice. Which is not very much. But
we cannot keep her out. She has the key and must learn for
herself why."

"What's going on?" Alice asked. If she was going to be
told she was rude again, she was going to at least try to speed
along the experience and get to the point so she could leave.

"Morgana is here."

Alice waited for him to continue. She watched as he took another deep drag of his hookah and continued to say nothing. Tiger Lily let out a low growl, but that did nothing to motivate him to say anything more. The smell of apples grew heavier around them.

"Is that bad?" Alice asked.

"Very."

This silence didn't last nearly as long. Tiger Lily would not stand for it, nor would she sit for it, and she spun around to face Alice. "Morgana is another queen in the castle," she said "She comes from another place. Not Wonderland. Not Neverland. She was not meant to escape and now that she has, she wishes to destroy both places. To do this, she will need many things, but she will eventually also need you and Peter. When she has both of you, she will be able to destroy both lands."

Alice looked from Tiger Lily to the Caterpillar, then back again. "How do either of you know this?" she asked. "She's been married and living in New York for years. Why would she want to come here and destroy a bunch of places she's never been to?"

"Don't be so presumptuous," Caterpillar snapped. "She is not so quick to know that yet. Always a little slow, that one.

Never knows what she's sitting on. But she will figure it out eventually. When she knows where we are and what it came from, she will do whatever it takes. Best to prevent her from achieving her goals before she knows what they are."

"But she might never know what they are," Alice said. "Do you know her?"

"It hasn't even been a moon since I saw her last," Caterpillar said. "She has always been far too ambitious for her own good, though women are so terribly slow. She may have had some talent, but not the strength of character..."

"You have started him again," Tiger Lily said, getting to her feet. "Come, he will never finish until he knows there is no one listening."

Alice looked back, but got to her feet and was more than happy to get out of there. The smell of apples was helping her headache, but it also gave her a sense of dread and making her very hungry. Thoughts of home came back, of the room she would have to go back to when she was done with the school year. She wondered if she could just stay in Wonderland over the break.

She wondered if Wonderland would still welcome her.

"Something strange is happening, Alice of Wonderland," Tiger Lily said. "Since the castle moved into the hole between the worlds, nothing has been the same. My people are changing. I can feel that I am becoming a different person. The

Caterpillar is the only one who has any explanation. He is strange, but he has always wanted Wonderland to be well and whole. Alice of Wonderland, this way."

If Wonderland didn't want her, then none of this would mean anything. She'd stay away and she would have to go back to school. And when she went back now, she was coming back with a different secret, one that she didn't even know she was holding for so long. If that's what was really happening.

Maybe she just needed to try harder. She could fall for someone if she tried really hard. She'd read enough books to know that it sometimes took a really long time to find the right one, and then you would know. It didn't matter that it didn't feel right. She just hadn't found the right person yet. That was all.

Someone at the castle might have answers for her. She did have a meeting...

Alice didn't realize she was wandering until Tiger Lily took her hand and tugged her onward. Alice looked down at the hand holding her. She was still thinking about home and the things she was going to have to think about again once she was back there.

"I am sorry, Alice of Wonderland," Tiger Lily continued. "I may not be myself for much longer and will not be able to continue to earn your forgiveness for much longer. Know that

I never intended any harm when I caused you pain. I only wanted to help my people."

"Didn't I already forgive you for that?" Alice asked. She should feel something right now. She should feel something when someone held her hand. But no matter who she imagined holding it right now, she couldn't even imagine feeling anything about it.

"I will never do enough to earn that," Tiger Lily said. "You forgive too easily, Alice of Wonderland. And now I must do something more that I apologize for."

Alice looked up at her, but was overcome with an image of her room. She barely knew what was going on when Tiger Lily took her hand away and putting it on a large mirror. Alice didn't know where it had come from, only that Tiger Lily swung it up and brought it down over Alice's head. Instinctively, Alice ducked and found herself falling head first out of Wonderland and into her dorm room.

CHAPTER 21

Heartless

ADAM FOLDED HIS feet under him, his fingers twirling a pen between them like it was a knife he was ready to throw at the door. Since getting back from Wonderland, there were habits that Adrianna couldn't help but notice. That place changed people, and Adrianna wasn't sure it was for the better.

Although, if she was honest, it hadn't changed Adam at all. It had just brought a few of his less kind qualities to the forefront. His quick anger, his lack of patience, his desire to do whatever he wanted no matter whom he hurt, those had refused to recede since he got back from Wonderland and Adrianna doubted they would ever go away now. Travis said it was only puberty, but he didn't even realize that Adam had been missing for two years, fighting a war that wasn't his to fight.

A war that was wearing Alice down while she was

only there part time. Why Adam wanted to go back was beyond her.

"Where's Alice?" he asked. He watched Adrianna as she went through the notes on her computer. Alice kept the books hidden, worried that someone else might slip into their room to steal them. She hadn't told Adrianna where they were, though Adrianna hadn't pressed. Adrianna wasn't sure she wanted to touch them herself too often if she didn't have to, and Alice kept very thorough notes.

"Wonderland," Adrianna told him. When he glared at her, she matched his look. "You always want her to go. You should be happy."

"She wasn't at Combat Club," he said.

"She went last night."

"Why?"

Adrianna took in a deep breath. She couldn't lie to him. She was just hoping he wouldn't ask, but here she was and there was nothing stopping her now. "I don't know. I think she was sleepwalking. She wasn't awake when she went through the mirror."

Adam didn't look happy about that answer, but he said nothing. Adrianna could guess what he was thinking. She could see it in the way he glowered at Alice's bed. He didn't like her, thought she wasn't spending *enough* time in Wonderland. He didn't see how worn down she was, how many bottles of painkillers she had gone through in only a week because Wonderland was pounding on the inside of her brain all the time. She would be happy to figure out some of these books if only so she could help ease some of that burden and let Alice have a little more normalcy.

If she could have thought of anyone else to come watch her practice magic, to make sure she wasn't going too far or losing her mind, she would have. She wasn't even sure if that was actually a thing that could happen, but Adrianna didn't like being alone while she did this. Didn't like being alone at all, if she was being honest.

"Adam?" she asked, a thought coming to her. Something Peter had said. That Alice hadn't told her. "If you could go back to Wonderland—"

"In a heartbeat," he told her, his eyes staring into hers. "They all suck there, but I'd actually stay long enough to save it."

That's what she thought. Adrianna nodded and went back through the notes. An easy one to start with. One that hadn't worked before, but that she'd already used to get Adam here.

"*Ábedecian Lance Michael Case hércyme.*" She could feel the tingle on her tongue to tell her something happened, but still she frowned at the words. "I still think the grammar's wrong."

"I don't like this, Addie," Adam said. "Those books are dangerous. She shouldn't have let you look at them."

"They're just books. Books don't hurt people. People do."

"Those books have hurt plenty of people," he insisted. He made a movement with the pen and stopped, as if only now realizing it was a pen and not something else. Frustrated, he put it down next to him. "*Those* books have destroyed lives."

Adrianna smiled at him. "I'll be careful," she said. "And I promise not to turn anyone into a zombie."

Adam wasn't smiling at that, letting out a grunt and fidgeting with his hands. He desperately wanted something back in them and Adrianna was almost certain that shouldn't happen. Adam wasn't the kind brother with a mean streak any longer. That mean streak was who he would be until he was allowed back to the other side of the mirror, and maybe even after he got that. She was grateful to Alice for bringing him back to her, and for insisting on not letting him rejoin whatever it was he was doing over there. She could only hope he never went back, though he wasn't entirely free of whatever grasp Wonderland held on him.

Arthur's words drifted back into her mind. A warning that she could not trust Adam. It was mirrored in how Sarah looked at him. She still didn't know what that meant and, in the silence stretching on between them, she thought to finally ask.

"Arthur said something to me about you a while ago,"

Adrianna said finally, watching Adam. "He doesn't seem to like you very much."

"He's a dick."

"Alice said something too."

"Ignore her," Adam told her. The response was automatic. His jaw set and he wouldn't meet her eyes, but there was something guilty about him in that moment. He was almost regretful and Adrianna didn't want the answer if it was going to upset him more than this.

"Okay," she said.

"How long is this going to take?" he asked. His words were sharp, but it was less anger than impatience now. She would have to be very careful if she wanted to find out what happened, but that could wait until another time. He wasn't ready to talk about it yet, but maybe one day.

Adrianna shrugged in response to the question. "As long as it takes to walk across campus, I think. It doesn't really make people appear. You're sure Arthur won't notice if he just leaves?"

"Heather's got him doing some stuff for Club today," Adam said. There was still venom on his tongue, but it was now familiar and manageable. Lance had once been able to temper him, but that wasn't the case any longer. Apparently Lance had barely even been around lately. "And I'm sure he'll take the chance to show off. He won't even notice Lance is missing."

Arianna didn't like the sound of that. Arthur wasn't nice to Alice when they encountered one another and Arthur wasn't going to be any nicer with a sword in his hand. Still, Arthur was distracted and Adam didn't seem too concerned. And, for whatever concerns Adrianna might have about Alice, Heather would make sure Alice wasn't hurt. If nothing else, she could probably expect that Alice and Peter would slip off again to have their own private Combat Club sessions as soon as Peter thought to ask.

Adam slipped into silence, his eyes firmly on the door at first before sliding back to Alice's bed. If it could have been Lance helping her, she would have welcomed it. She didn't know how to deal with Adam and his anger. His resentment. His drive to go back to a place that had brought out the worst in him.

"So it takes sleepwalking to make her do what she's supposed to."

"No one should be going to Wonderland if we can help it," Adrianna told him. "It's *dangerous*."

"It's her responsibility," Adam told her. His voice had lost the edge and the anger as he said it, more like he was reciting something for class. "Wonderland chose her to do it. If she would just stay there and fix things, she could have been done by now. Instead she's getting mixed up with..." He stopped himself, frowning and shaking his head. "It could have been done by now."

"That's not fair," Adrianna insisted. "She can't just leave everything to go there. People notice she's missing."

"Like they noticed I went missing?" he asked. "Or Matt?"

"That's not fair."

"It doesn't have to be. It's true."

Adrianna had nothing to say to that and went quiet. Adam picked up the pen again and made it look deadly as he toyed with it in his hands. She hadn't really paid much mind when Matt and Adam had gone missing. Or when Lance had. The resentment wasn't entirely unwarranted, but it still felt unfair. She had been so certain they would come back. Claudia made sure they were all so certain about that.

She blinked. "What happened to Claudia?" Adrianna asked. "I know she left, but..."

Confusion passed over Adam's face as well, but a knock interrupted them. Lance flung the door open and looked at the pair with an expression that was very unlike himself. He grinned, shaking his head like he had caught the pair. "Door open, kiddos," he told him. "Related or no, boys in the girls dorms is very unseemly."

"What is *wrong* with you?" Adam asked. His glare went all over Lance, trying to find any explanation. "*Unseemly?*"

"What's wrong is..." Lance frowned, his forehead creasing as he looked around. "Why am I here?" he asked.

"You missed your family?" Adrianna suggested. "It's been a while since we've talked."

"Why would I want to talk to you guys?" he asked. "You're all about Wonderland these days. I've moved on. There's no..."

Confusion gave way to something else as he paced around the room. He went to Alice's bed and put one hand on the end of it. "Oh, that's not right," he muttered, sagging himself back down onto it.

"You okay?" Adrianna asked. She got to her feet, watching him carefully and getting carefully closer, creeping on him like he might run.

It was clear as she got closer that he was in no condition to run at all. He leaned forward, his skin pale and eyes unfocused as he looked at nothing. His left arm went slack next to him. He dropped heavily in a lump, trying to aim for the bed. He went off the side of it and tumbled like a rag doll to the ground. He landed with a thud and inhaled a deep, gasping breath.

Adam was on his feet, eyes wide and panicked as he watched. His hands were out in front of him, but he had no idea what he was supposed to do as his brother took another gulp of air. Lance brought his right hand up to his chest and spread it over the middle. He looked at no one as his eyes searched the ceiling, searching for either of them and finding nothing. He was twitching, more and more weakly with each passing moment.

Adrianna and Adam watched, both creeping forward and scared to touch him. Adrianna didn't know what was happening or what she was supposed to do. Her breath caught in her throat. Her skin was hot, but inside was frozen and she couldn't move, staring and hoping desperately that Adam would figure out what they needed to do.

"Taken," Lance managed to whisper. And then he went very still.

Adam froze, his eyes going wildly between Adrianna and Lance lying motionless on the floor.

Adrianna didn't know what was making her move as she jumped off her bed and rushed over to Lance. She could barely see, her eyes watering and her brother blurry before her. He wasn't moving and she had to do *something*. She didn't know what she was supposed to do, how to check for a pulse or when she should see if she could pry open his eyes.

"Lance?" she said, her voice far too loud and far too high. Behind her, Adam had decided the most important thing right now was to close the door. "Lance!" She shook him, but he didn't move or get up.

"Arthur's coming," Adam warned her.

Adrianna didn't pay that any attention. Her hand went to his chest where Lance's still rested. He was so cold and she hesitated to move it. Gently, she tapped it and saw it dip into his shirt for a second. Directly into his chest.

Gently, Adrianna pressed her fingers into Lance's shirt next to his hand. She couldn't feel his ribs under the shirt, but something elastic instead. She pressed again and her fingers sprang back up. Eyes wide, she backed away just enough to tear up his shirt to see what was there.

"Addie, what are you—"

Adam stopped as they both saw what he'd been hiding. Under his shirt, there was a band of elastic bandages wrapped around Lance's chest. It only covered half of it, the bottom revealing a hole in his chest where his heart should be. Instead, there was only darkness, the likes of which should not be inside a person.

"Taken," Adam repeated, eyes wide and terrified.

"Oh my god," Adrianna said. It didn't make sense. This couldn't be happening. Her brother couldn't be like this. It shouldn't be possible. *He couldn't.*

His heart was gone. It hit Adrianna so suddenly that it left her dizzy. Her brother had been walking around without a heart and she didn't know it. She didn't even know how long he had been like this. And now they had killed him entirely by accident. Questions circled her mind trying to figure out how long he'd been without and if she could have noticed that he was dying any sooner. If there had been any way to prevent this. If there was any chance to bring him back.

And then his closed eyes squeezed tighter shut. Lance's head started to move and he came far too suddenly back to life. Adrianna was frozen, watching. He couldn't move. He didn't have a heart. There was no way—

Adam took his shirt and yanked it back into place, hauling Adrianna away from him. From the other side of the room, they watched as Lance stirred. He came back to life and got to his feet like nothing had happened. Lance looked at the pair, eyes narrowed and suspicious.

"What's wrong with you two?" he asked.

They both stared at him, neither saying a word. Adam held Adrianna close and away from Lance, pen in one hand. Adrianna struggled to understand what was going on. Lance didn't have a heart. He was dead only a second ago. He couldn't be alive again. But he couldn't be dead either.

None of this could be happening.

Arthur leaned into the room, grinning and looking from Adrianna to Lance. He gave her a wink before his attention went to Lance. "Hey, you coming?"

"Later." Lance grinned in a way that wasn't like him at all before he joined Arthur and left.

"We need to get Alice," Adam told her. "*Now.*"

CHAPTER 22

Interference and Answers

ADRIANNA BARELY SLEPT, constantly looking at the mirror for some sign of Alice coming back, but eventually the fatigue took her and she finally got some rest. When her bed was empty in the morning, she panicked again, worried that she had missed her, but she quickly told herself that wasn't so. Her coat was still draped over the back of her chair, and it was much too cold for her to go out without it.

It was probably for the best, she decided. Lance was... He wasn't well. She needed to figure out how to make him better, but he'd survived for this long like this. According to Adam, so long as he stayed near Arthur maybe they would have time. Whatever Arthur was doing, he was keeping Lance okay for now.

She needed to learn more magic. All of Alice's notes, she had to go through them and figure them out. There was no way she wasn't going to help Alice get Lance's heart back now. And that was what she had to do. That was missing. And there was only one place it could be.

Adrianna picked up her phone, ready to look up spells, when she saw the alert. She said she would meet Kevin and Rob for lunch today didn't she? They wanted to try something in town and no one else was free today. She'd also said she would bring Alice along but, clearly, that wouldn't happen today. With a sigh, Adrianna got up and got herself together before rushing into town, hoping she wasn't too late.

It was a new dessert shop, specializing in cookies and cakes, called Bakeology. Kevin and Rob were already sitting in a blue booth side by side, leaving the other side open for Adrianna to join them. They stopped talking as soon as they spotted her, waving her over, though Kevin was still typing on his phone.

"No Alice?" Rob asked. He wasn't unkind about it, smiling as he said it.

"She's just—"

"Don't want to know," Rob insisted. "If I know, I'll have to get involved. And I don't want to get involved."

"Heather's not that bad," Kevin insisted, frowning at his phone.

"I beg to differ. Everything okay?"

Kevin let out a breath through his pursed lips and put the phone face down next to him. "Probably," he said. "Peter's stopped going missing at least, but he thinks he... smells bad." There was something unspoken in the way he said it and in the way he carefully avoided looking at Adrianna.

"But with Alice missing and Peter accounted for, we can finally put to rest the idea that the two of them are a thing, right?" Rob said, nudging Kevin lightly.

"I can guarantee you that they weren't ever a thing," she insisted.

"You say that like she tells you everything," Kevin said. "She keeps a lot of secrets, or haven't you noticed?"

Adrianna only smiled in response. There was very little she could say to convince him otherwise. Alice wouldn't talk about Wonderland and Adrianna wouldn't betray that, even if she didn't like what was happening. Now that Alice wasn't keeping journals of her journeys to the other side and had hidden the ones she'd written before somewhere new, Adrianna didn't have any way of knowing what was going on over there and relied on Alice to tell her.

Not that it was working well anymore.

"While you're here, do you know what the deal is with Lance?" Rob asked. "We were working on something and he's just completely ghosted me."

Adrianna shook her head. "Sorry. I haven't even talked to

him much." She wasn't even sure where to start with Lance right now.

"Just... let me know," he said.

Adrianna nodded. From the concern on his face and the way he kept glancing at Kevin, Adrianna didn't want to press for more right now. "I'm going to get something," she said, getting up from the booth to look through the cake options. She wanted to dwell on that a little longer, but didn't want to tell either of them what was going on. That Alice wasn't really telling her as much anymore. That she wanted to believe her, but there was something in the way she kept the information short that made Adrianna think she was keeping something from her. That she was worried she was in over her head.

Not that Alice was the biggest of her concerns anymore. It felt almost wrong to be here instead of figuring out what she was going to do about Lance.

Adrianna looked at her phone, taking a few photos of the cakes and thinking about posting them. Two drew her: One covered in pink flower icing stating that it was Rose Decadence and the other a chocolate peanut butter that was the same price. She looked through her phone, finding just what she wanted and pocketed it before ordering the chocolate peanut butter with a cup of tea.

They got it to her quickly on a small silver tray. Adrianna

turned away with it, trying to hold one spell in her mind. Quietly, she spoke an incantation, imagining this cake was the other one. In front of her eyes, the cake changed, the smooth chocolate growing pink and textured as the flower icing grew. The cake went pale until it was a vanilla specked with rose.

When she sat down, she took a bite and confusion spread from inside her mouth to her face. It still tasted like chocolate peanut butter.

"Not good?" Kevin asked.

"It's good!" Adrianna said. She couldn't look at either of them, feeling the colour rising in her cheeks. She didn't like feeling like she was misleading them, but the truth might not be the best thing right now. "Just not what I was expecting."

"Can I try some?"

"Heads up," Rob said, his eyes firmly on the door. "Your stalker is back."

Adrianna didn't need him to tell her that. She could hear her brother and Arthur laughing as soon as they came in the door like there was nothing wrong. Like everything was perfectly fine and like it had always been. Like Lance wasn't now hiding a gaping hole in his chest where his heart should be.

Somehow, Arthur was keeping him alive, that much was clear to her, though she didn't know how he did it. That final moment before Lance had died right in front of her, that flicker over his face where he looked like himself, that concerned her the most. It was like he was being locked away inside himself, like Arthur had put someone else in place of her brother.

She needed to get his heart back so she could get her brother back. But first, she needed to have a word with Arthur.

"I'll be right back," Adrianna said, getting up from the booth, leaving her purse behind. "Watch my stuff?"

"You don't have to do this right now," Rob warned her.

"Do what?"

Kevin smacked him lightly on the arm. "It's Addie. She won't."

"Do what?" she repeated.

"He thinks you're finally going to tell him off for following you around."

"Oh," she said, considering. "I mean, I already asked him to stop and he's doing it less now? But that's not what—"

"You weren't even thinking about—"

"She was absolutely not thinking about it," Kevin confirmed. His eyes danced, watching as she smiled apologetically. He reached over to take another bite of his cake and pushed his plate toward Rob to distract him.

Lance looked tired as he sat across from Arthur. He'd looked tired for a while, but now Adrianna really noticed it wearing on him at the edges. He was still smiling, the corners of his mouth pulling in a way that was too much like Adam and not enough like himself. There was a cruelty and a lack of caring about other people that hadn't been there before and, if Adam hadn't been so changed physically by Wonderland, they would now probably be very hard to tell apart.

"We need to talk," Adrianna told Arthur, her eyes lingering a little longer on her brother before going back to him.

"Take a seat," Arthur said. "Lance, go make yourself busy somewhere else."

Lance didn't hesitate to get up and out of the way. He presented the vacant seat to Adrianna, smiling much too wide. Her stomach felt like a brick as she took the seat. She watched as he meandered over to see Kevin and Rob, waving and sliding into the booth with them.

"You're keeping him alive, aren't you?" Her eyes cut back to him and cut through whatever comment he had ready.

"So long as I keep him close by he'll live, don't worry." "Thank you for saving him." Even if he was doing it for his own reasons, and Adrianna was under no illusions about that, it was worth saying she was grateful that her brother wasn't dead. One had already been lost and may never be brought back, she would like to make sure she didn't lose another.

"It's gotten a lot harder since you snatched him away, though. If you want to keep him alive for much longer, you're going to need to not do that anymore, Addie."

The sound of that name on his tongue sent an uncomfortable twinge up her spine. It was what everyone called her, but hearing him say it made her feel uncomfortable. Those piercing eyes weren't doing anything to ease her discomfort, not even when they softened.

"It's not so bad," Arthur said. "I'm more than happy to help. Show you I'm not so bad as some other people might tell you I am. I really am a very reasonable person."

"How long have you been doing that?" she asked, glancing back at the booth. Lance had them thoroughly distracted, no matter how they tried to look around them, though Kevin managed a very concerned glance in her direction. "When did he lose it?"

"About a month ago," he told her easily. "We met the Queen of Hearts and she was quite keen on it. I think she might have mistaken him for his prick of a brother. Damn woman thinks she's a queen just because she has a castle. False monarchs don't belong on the throne. They've done nothing to earn it."

Adrianna nodded, taking in a contemplative breath. That would make more sense. Adam had caused more trouble, and Alice had mentioned in her journals she had seen a box made just for Adam's heart somewhere in the Queen's skirts. "Adam," she muttered, only a little annoyed about it.

"It really has gotten a lot more difficult to keep him alive," Arthur said. His hand crept across the table to graze hers. "If you could get Alice to fetch his heart back, I would appreciate it. Or if you could stop trying to take him so far away. The longer his body is properly dead, the harder it is to keep him moving. As it is, I should really ask a favour to continue for all the trouble."

Her eyes stayed on his, but a part of her was looking at his face and wondering what it would be like to feel that strong jaw under her fingers. He wanted to be with her, that much he made very clear. She wanted to say no, knew that no amount of beauty in the face could undo everything else about him. That he was currently threatening to kill her brother to make her more pliable. But staring into those eyes, she could almost forget...

But she couldn't fully forget that he was following her wherever she went. That he had said and done such horrible things to Alice. That he had once turned her brother into a dog and already stolen a kiss from her. Couldn't forget that he was only keeping Lance alive so he could get close to her and now threatening her with it.

She could say yes. She could just say yes.

Adrianna sucked in a breath and pulled her hands away from him. "Thank you," she said, her mind racing as her heart was pounding in her chest. "You've kept him alive for this long. But I think it might be best for everyone if we try to get his heart back."

"We?" Arthur looked amused as he watched her.

"Alice is the only one who can put the hearts back."

He let out a small grunt, only partially amused. Red flashed across his face before he put the mischievous smile back on his face and inched closer to her again. "I meant what you intended to do," he said, implying Adrianna as he spoke. "I was under the impression that you did not dirty your fair hands with Wonderland."

Adrianna was calm and smiled kindly. "I think it's about time the Queen of Hearts was stopped, don't you? False monarchs don't belong on the throne, right?"

CHAPTER 23

Storm the Castle

WHEN SHE LANDED back on their bedroom floor
Monday morning, Adrianna wasted no time in telling Alice
about everything that had happened while she was away.
Lance didn't have a heart. They needed to go back right
now to try and get it back. She was already assembling the
people they would need to make sure the Queen of Hearts
would never do anything like this again. They would go this
weekend, giving Adrianna a little more time to get more
comfortable with the magic she was now studying very
closely.

Alice hadn't even noticed Lance was different. She played
that last trip to Wonderland with him over in her head and
she could figure out when Lance must have lost his heart.
Arthur had been distracted when he insisted they went back.
She should have known, but there was nothing she could do.

Even if she got his heart back, she didn't know how she would get it back into him. Especially not now.

And she had told Adrianna she was getting better. She was going to have to tell her soon that she couldn't even think of the spell anymore without getting dizzy. Maybe if she tried hard enough she could make herself do it, but somehow Alice knew something had changed. Whatever had stopped her before had gotten stronger.

It would have been easier if no one was going with Alice, if Adrianna hadn't insisted on being part of it. If it hadn't been Adrianna's brother and she wasn't determined to help. If she weren't bringing together even more people. Adrianna had been reading the books so much lately that Alice wondered if Adrianna could put the hearts back instead, but Alice couldn't do that to her. It wasn't up to Adrianna to do that. No matter how much she wanted to, it was Alice who had to finish doing that for Wonderland.

Not to mention this was Adrianna. She would not be able to handle the hearts.

Friday night came too soon. Adrianna had barely eaten dinner, too anxious for what was coming. She had packed and unpacked a bag several times over the week before Alice told her there would be no need for it. She brought Adam's coat out of storage, disliking that he was coming at all. Adrianna didn't seem to understand that Adam would try to stay, but by Friday Adrianna had been too determined to listen and Alice was feeling too guilty about letting this happen at all to argue.

"Who else are we waiting for?" she asked, looking around at who was here. Adam looked downright surly at the question while Adrianna was going through Alice's notes on her phone. "I think someone's going to notice you're gone," she told Adrianna. It wasn't too late for her to turn back.

"It'll be okay," Adrianna insisted. "I'll just tell them I was with you."

"Or that this was a family matter," Adam added. "Also technically true."

Adrianna smiled brighter before taking the last of the notes. "Arthur's bringing Lance," she said. "You might not be able to put hearts back if you're not in Wonderland."

"Why not?" This was the first time she'd heard of that.

"I don't want to take any chances," Adrianna said. "You've never done it outside of Wonderland before, right? It might be a thing you can only do there."

"Because Wonderland is inherently *wrong*," Arthur said, appearing in the door and looking pompous next to a playful Lance. Today the end of his left sleeve was pinned up and Arthur had abandoned his prosthetic. Adam glowered and looked away. He couldn't make himself look too long at the corrupted version of his brother. "You can't live without your heart even in Neverland. Not for long. Not until Wendy puts another one in you."

"Lance is still standing."

"By my favour alone," Arthur said. "And it's tiring. Let's get this over with. I'll be happy to not have to work so hard on this anymore."

Alice turned back to the mirror. One by one, they passed into Wonderland and arrived in the White Rabbit's house.

THE WHITE RABBIT was not alone, but he wasn't with company either. The bodies moved about the house to clean as he stared at the parade of people coming through the mirror, finally stopping Alice when she appeared. "I say, terribly impolite to invite yourself and so many others to another person's house without so much as a consult!"

"Only passing through," Alice told him.

"This is my *home* not a *highway!*"

Adrianna paused at that. She opened her mouth to say something, closed it, and let her demeanour change to apologetic before she opened it again. "We're very sorry for the intrusion. We'll be on our way and let you get back to your day."

"I should hardly think this is your fault, dear," the White Rabbit told her, turning his eyes back on Alice.

Alice could hardly find herself offended anymore. The White Rabbit knew full well that she was going to continue using his mirror. It was the safest place, and a good place to leave people if they got cold feet. She thought that the White Rabbit wouldn't mind. So far he had been gracious enough to continue to allow them to move back and forth as they pleased. It was strange that he would be mentioning it now.

"Go ahead," Alice said. "I'll be right there."

Adrianna turned sharply back as Adam led the way. "Are you sure?"

Alice nodded and offered her a small smile. She didn't look convinced, but she followed her brothers and Arthur out the door.

Alice waited until the door was closed before she spoke. "May I no longer use your mirror?" she asked.

"*You* I have permitted," he told her sharply. "The rest, I am uncertain. There must be a certain vetting process before one simply allows another to walk into your house. That is what a door is for. And I must say, you have brought many dangerous friends into my house."

"Only dangerous to me," she pointed out.

"That is hardly a comfort. Perhaps you need to install a door to your acquaintance and ask them their name before you let them into your life."

"Wonderland needs the door more right now, I'd say. It's already letting a lot of people in that it's not checking first."

"That's hardly the point," Rabbit said, but he was softening, his rigid fur tamping down into much softer fluff. "I will forgive you for now, though I will request that you come first and ask for permission from your guests in the future. If you do not, I will soon require it."

Alice smiled, unbidden, at that. "Understood," she said. "Thank you for your graciousness."

"And you must come by for tea," he said. "We have some things to discuss. You and I and that cat. We have business that we must deal with."

"Another time," Alice said. They were likely getting away from her at this point. "I must catch up with my party. We need to rescue a heart."

"That is your task," the White Rabbit said by way of a goodbye. "Good that you are returning to it."

Alice nodded before she left, thinking of Adam's coat and going to meet it.

THEY WASTED NO time getting across Wonderland and to the castle, following the great crevice in the sky and the smattering of stars dotting the darkness. Everything was still around the stone walls of the castle, though there was no shortage of people. It was strange to see so many people, the combination of woodland creatures, playing cards, and humans, all of them with gaping holes in their chests and standing in perfectly straight lines, motionlessly staring out into Wonderland. She had no idea just how many people were actually there.

Lance went ahead, looking closer at the front line and peering at them like they were guards, waving his hand in front of their faces. "Do these guys actually do anything?" he asked, his face getting uncomfortably close to one of the cards and his hand looking like he was ready to give it a shove.

"Get away from there," Adam snapped at him.

"You gonna make me?"

"If I have to."

"He's not himself," Adrianna warned him, looking back and forth between her brothers. She looked like she wanted to say more, but her eyes trailed to Arthur. He didn't meet her gaze, shaking his head at the lines and letting out a sigh.

"If they aren't going to move anyway," he said, eyes narrowing and glowering at the line in front of him. He already looked tired as he brought his right hand up in front of him. He snapped, a clumsy action that he wasn't used to, and it took Alice a moment to realize just what he had done.

In front of them, the humans of the guard had shifted, changed into much smaller woodland creatures. There were only about five of them that had altered at all, none breaking rank or looking remotely bothered by their new forms. They still stood at attention, looking ahead and waiting for something to come in front of them.

"How the hell is that supposed to help?" Adam asked dryly, his hand going to his waist and plucking along the nothing he had to prepare for a fight.

"You can't just change someone like that," Alice noted. "It's rude to do so without their request. They might not want to be changed."

Arthur stared at Alice. "Are you being serious?" he asked, bewilderment overtaking him before the anger started to raise in his voice. "How do you expect to get in without dealing with this first?"

"Well, time to have some fun," Lance said, smiling. "Come on, first to a hundred? Not like they're going to fight back."

"You can't just *kill* them!" Adrianna said, horrified as the boys all went to their weapons. She tugged Adam back. "They aren't themselves! It's not fair!"

"Nothing about this is *fair,* Addie."

"Alice!" Adrianna said, turning back to her. "Isn't there another way?"

But Alice's attention was on the parapets of the castle, looking up at a woman standing above them all and looking down at them with a quizzical expression. She recognized

Claudia standing there, dressed in strange garb. No, she went by Morgana now. She had forgotten Morgana was here. She was supposed to go talk to her.

"Is that Claudia?" Adrianna asked next to her.

"Morgana." The word came out like a curse from Arthur and he glowered back up at her, the concentration returning to his face. He grabbed Lance and they plunged into the first line of guards, all of them coming to life now that someone had tried to cross their lines. Adrianna jumped back and tried to stay out of the way, looking horrified at the fight breaking out around her.

"I need to go," Alice said. "I'll be back." She took one step forward and she was gone.

CHAPTER 24

A Fair Chance

ADRIANNA WAS CAUGHT between surprise at seeing Claudia again after so long, shock that Lance was plunging into a fight, and concern as Alice vanished. She didn't even hear what Alice said, too concerned with making sure that the fight didn't get too close. She had nothing that might save her from a sword — a far too real sword — that might threaten to hurt her. Nothing to defend herself. She should have figured out armour of some sort, but she wasn't sure that would make her heart pound any less or make her feel any less frozen in place as the battle spread around her.

Adam flew out of it and picked her up, dragging her away. "Was that Claudia?" he asked, his eyes going back to crawl over the battle. Lance and Arthur worked their way through the ranks, vanishing into the castle. In front of her, the remaining people stepped over their fallen to reform the lines again.

"I can't do this," she muttered into his shoulder.

"Go back then," he told her, putting her down. "Find Tiger Lily. She'll take care of you. I need to make sure Arthur doesn't—"

"Adam," Adrianna said, eyes wide as she watched the people lining the castle part. There was something both smooth and mechanical about it, like dancers that had long ago grown bored with the routine. In the middle emerging from the castle, a knight dressed in pure white armour appeared on a white steed, trotting towards them.

"Run," Adam said, grabbing Adrianna by the arm and pulling her back toward the Native encampment. Adrianna tried to keep up with his long strides, seeing his frustration and feeling it in how he dragged her along. He forced himself to slow down and wouldn't let go of her as he tried to drag both of them onward to safety. She understood the alarm in his voice echoing through the one word, caught the panic in his eye, but that wasn't all she knew.

Behind them, the trot quickly became a gallop and the gallop was much too close for them to possibly escape on foot. Adam groped at his waist, looking for something that Alice had probably long since removed to keep him from trying to escape.

The knight reached down and grabbed Adam by the back of the coat, tossing him over the back of his horse with a thud.

Adam let go of Adrianna's arm and she dropped to the ground with a thump. She only got a moment to breathe in the scent of the strangely scentless Wonderland grass. Before she knew fully what was happening, something else grabbed her by the arms and hauled her to her feet.

Adam let out a cry of protest for only a moment before he went limp across the back of the horse, not unconscious but clearly much too incapacitated to protest any longer. Adrianna wondered just how many times he'd suffered a concussion while he was here. She wondered just how many injuries this place had given her family. It was the worst kind of wonder.

"We didn't go across the line," Adrianna said Alice had talked about how talking had sometimes gotten her out of things. Reasoning with them with whatever reason she could come up with. "Why are you taking us if we didn't cross the line?"

"This one belongs to the Queen of Hearts," he said. "He and any accomplices. You are my prisoners now. Come. You would not care to fight me."

Adrianna didn't know what else to say. Her eyes strayed to a long sword at his side, the blade steel and sharp. She didn't want to fight him at all.

ADRIANNA TRIED TO remind herself that this was

exactly what she wanted. She wanted to see the Queen of Hearts. She wanted to give her a chance to explain why she had done that to her brother. Wanted to understand. Wanted to get her brother's heart back. But this was not how she wanted things to go.

The throne room was large and plush, full of people standing and staring straight ahead with no expression as the Queen of Hearts stood at her throne. A man was sitting next to her, dressed all in red and with a distinct sag in the fabric around his chest. Everyone around them had that, none of them still in possession of their hearts. The Queen had claimed them all.

She was beautiful, but there was a wickedness to her that Adrianna could not miss. A madness in those eyes as Adrianna was pushed forward by her trading card guards. Next to her, the white knight carried Adam over his shoulder and dropped him to the ground at the Queen's feet. He curled in on himself, clutching his head and trying to pull himself to his feet. When he got his legs under him, the knight clubbed him once more with the pommel of his sword to keep him down.

The Queen's eyes narrowed on the white knight, then on Adam. "I already took this one," she said dismissively. "Toss him in the dungeons."

"He ran," the White Knight said.

Adrianna tried to move forward, but the cards held her tight. She didn't know what she was planning to do, only that she didn't want the Queen to get too close to him. Her body wouldn't move, frozen by everything happening as the Queen knelt down and picked Adam up by the chin.

"Bitch." The word was quiet, barely spoken at all, but it echoed in the silence of a room filled with so many people.

She bent down to speak to Adam, her voice too quiet to hear but it was surely something cruel. Her lips curled up in a smile as she spoke. Adam could clearly hear her, trying to get up enough to fight back, but his fierce look was dulled by the fog in his eyes from the number of times he had been hit in the head.

"Far too long," the Queen told him more loudly, riding up to her full height. With her back straight, a delicate scowl crossed her features and she brought a single hand up in front of her face. She murmured something, not in the old English that Alice had been using but in something that felt much more made up.

Slowly, out of the tip of her pointer finger, a long porcelain claw grew from her nail, ending in a long hook. Adrianna's eyes grew wide, having heard enough about this to know exactly what to expect. Alice told her of the long porcelain claw that speared many hearts. She hadn't seen it herself before, but it appeared in her nightmares. She never wanted to see it happening for real, and not to her brother.

"No!" Adrianna knew what was coming and she couldn't

just sit by and let it happen. Tears stung her eyes and she felt helpless, but she had to do *something*. Alice could figure out what to do here, but she wasn't Alice. She didn't know how this world worked, no matter the stories. Asking? Alice said that worked, right? "Please don't hurt him."

The malicious look on the Queen's face softened into confusion for only a moment. "Anything worth doing will hurt, my dear," she told Adrianna. "Pain is a natural part of the essentials of life. Why, I've spent many days in great emotional pains over this one's actions."

"You're going to kill him," she pleaded with her.

"Shut up, Addie," Adam shot at her. His look was too bleary to focus on her, but he was desperate for her to be quiet, even as he was so quiet himself. She hated seeing him like this and struggled to free herself to go to him, but the cards held her in place.

A derisive noise escaped her pursed lips. "I am only taking his heart, not his head. And I am the Queen of Hearts. His heart is rightfully mine. As, I will remind you, is yours."

Adrianna's eyes went wide as the Queen turned her attention to her and that long claw came to study her. "You can't," she said, now trying to back away, but again the cards held her in place. Her mind was racing, the image of her heart on the end of that spike now racing through her mind. She didn't like it here. It was horrifying. And Alice, how did Alice manage it? Why would Adam ever want to come back here?

"You will find I can do what I please," the Queen told her. But the claw strayed, going up further to brush at Adrianna's cheek. The tears had leaked out and the claw caressed one of those, a look of disgust overtaking the Queen. "Hm," she said shortly, regarding Adrianna again. "I had hoped that perhaps I finally found a pretty daughter, but you will need work as well. You have turned much too red and watery. But that's nothing a little paint won't fix."

Adrianna's heart pounded in her chest and the words died on her lips. She didn't want to be here. She wanted none of this. She wanted to go back to school, where everything was normal and she was doing anything but this. She shouldn't have come. She couldn't remember why she had come. This was a mistake. Alice was right. Wonderland was no place for her.

"But first, we must remember proper order," the Queen said. "It will not do to forget our manners at such a time. You will have your turn."

Adrianna barely registered what she said, the fear overtaking her as the Queen's claw and attention left her. Instead, she turned back to Adam and gently flicked her wrist. The claw grew suddenly longer out the tip of her finger in a curve and pierced through Adam's back and appeared out his chest, hitting the ground with a tiny click.

Adam's scream was anything but quiet.

Adrianna's eyes flew wide, suddenly very aware of everything that was happening around her. Suddenly very aware that her brother was dying in front of her to the hands of a queen and under the watchful eye of the court. This was not how it was supposed to go. She should be able to talk her way through this. Alice had always said she could talk her way through anything that happened in Wonderland. No words were enough here.

Not even the words of the spell she had planned. It felt mean to do before without giving the Queen of Hearts a fair chance to do the right thing. Now it didn't seem cruel enough.

"*Tólýsing!*" She yanked her arms down sharply and freed herself, though she didn't move, planting her feet as the castle trembled. She almost didn't know what she was doing as her hands moved, as she made her intent known. It was more of a feeling than anything else, a need to make her stop and to protect her family. The Queen of Hearts let out her own wail and there was a crack as the nail broke from the rest of her finger. She tried to move, but already her feet had turned to stone. Followed soon by the rest of her.

But that was not enough. The vines grew out of nowhere, breaking through the ground of the throne room and overtaking the room around them. They came for the Queen of Hearts first, encasing her in a web of leaves and branches, of vines that grew roses covered in thorns and a bramble that would be too thick for anyone to dare enter again.

The surrounding flowers kept growing, larger and larger and through the roof. The cards and people of the court did not move, not so much as side stepping the flowers as they knocked them aside. They grew around Adrianna and Adam, up into the warring sky above the castle. They took the power that the Queen of Hearts had gained and drew from her as the source, growing far up into the sky until they filled the hole that the castle had made in Wonderland.

CHAPTER 25

Negotiations

ALICE WASN'T SURE where she was going. The halls all blended into one another, though that might be because she kept going down the same three halls over and over again, hoping that she didn't miss the appearance of a door she needed to go through. It would help if she could remember who she was supposed to meet here and why. It would also help if people didn't keep appearing in every hall she walked down shortly after she appeared there. It was making it very difficult to look for what she was supposed to find.

Hands grabbed her around the shoulders and spun her around until she was looking at Arthur. "Where is she?" he demanded.

"She?" Alice asked. "I'm a she and I am here."

"She's not wrong," Lance said, a wide grin on his face as he held Alice in front of him.

"Don't you start," Arthur snapped, though Alice wasn't sure who it was directed at. He looked furious, his face flushing red from the neck and jaw clenched as he looked wildly back and forth down the hall. "Where did she go. You know where she went," he said, turning back to Alice and pointing the sword tip at her. "Morgana. Where is she?"

"In the place where she is," Alice said, pushing the sword aside and frowning. "No need to threaten me. I'll tell you what you want."

"Where. Is. She."

Alice let out an irritated breath. "This way," she told him, stepping away from the newly raised sword and heading down the hall. "No need to be so rude about it," she muttered. "I think she might be this way."

"I don't know which of these worlds is worse."

"This one," Lance told him. "I keep telling you, it's definitely this one."

Alice glanced back at him. There was none of Lance's apprehension when he said that, but that was definitely his sentiment showing through. She wasn't sure how much of it was him left and how much of him was whatever Arthur was doing.

"The other one has my hand," he said.

"And you aren't getting it back. Just let it go and move on."

"I'm getting really sick of you two right about now."

Lance let out a good natured sigh and laughed. "One of these days, you gotta learn when to quit. All these grudges you keep holding, you've gotta drop them before they swallow you whole. Maybe look into moving on and stop dwelling in the past."

"Don't make me regret bringing you back, Lancelot," Arthur said warningly.

"I never asked you to. You could have dragged Percival back from his slumber. But you don't have any reason to punish him for resting peacefully, do you?"

Alice was getting the distinct impression that she was missing something, but she stayed quiet. She had a lot of practice staying quiet now. The less she said, it seemed, the more she might learn.

But the hall was growing much too short. They had to get Lance's heart back, and she wondered if Lance would still be able to answer her questions when he was himself again. If this Lancelot had really taken him over completely and if Arthur would let Lance come back at all.

"Percival didn't betray me."

"Perhaps not, but this seems a little much. And that besides, you may have dragged me back, but your replacement consort likes you about as much as the original one did," Lance said.

"This one," Alice said. Somehow, the door felt right, though she could not say why. There was no way for her to know, no sign on it to say she was expected. Whoever wanted to speak to her was very inconsiderate. "Probably."

Arthur gripped his sword and Lance took up his own. Alice got out of the way and let them charge through the door first. She wanted to tell them a knock would have sufficed, but they were already through. She waited outside, peering in and waiting for Arthur to cause enough of a distraction before she decided to join them in there. It did not take long.

"You should have stayed dead," Arthur said, his sword in front of him and his left arm twitching. It did so for only a moment before he remembered that hand was left behind at Lucena Academy.

"So it really is you," Lance said, eyes narrowing on Morgana. He opened his mouth to say more, but kept it shut a moment later, a grin crossing his face, all too knowing. "I thought you were dead too."

"Times change," she said, her eyes not leaving Arthur and a flash of anger on her face. Arthur's stance changed ever so slightly, his face screwing up in protest, but Morgana continued like he was only a mild annoyance. "But it looks like you haven't. What do you think Lance Case did to you?"

Alice didn't catch the words that came out of Arthur's mouth next, only the smoke that filled the room. Her eyes went wide, staring into everything and trying to determine what was happening. She couldn't tell who was doing what, only that Morgana and Arthur appeared to be taking the opportunity to go at one another's throats. The clash was clear, even if Alice couldn't quite make out what the sounds meant, only that they were deafening.

Still, they were distracted and this was not what they were here for. Amidst the smoke, flowers and branches grew out of the ground. They encircled the center of the room, grabbing the smoke and pulled it in. The sound faded down into a few sparse curses as Arthur protested whatever was happening to him and Morgana sounded almost like she was singing.

And then it was quiet. A large dome of vines and flowers filled the middle of the room, spreading out to touch the high ceilings and bulging in parts to graze the walls. Alice could hear nothing of what was happening inside of it beyond a dull thud now and then. Otherwise, there was nothing.

"Lance?" Alice asked tentatively into the silence.

"Find the heart?" he asked in return. He sounded further away and the sound of rummaging had already begun. "Yeah. I'll see if it's over here."

Alice started going through what she could get to, trying to figure out where a heart might have been put. It felt like that room in Adrianna's house, with the plants that were hanging and drying, but now with so many more strange concoctions around the room. On the shelves were more herbs that she hadn't seen before and potions that smelled strange when she got close. There were trinkets that Alice was certain wasn't meant to be there, that had come from no corner of Wonderland or Neverland, but she could not think of another place it could have come from.

She had to find Lance's heart so that Lance could come back to life. It was so strange that the boy searching with her was not really Lance at all.

"Why did he call you Lancelot?" she asked.

"Because that's my name," he said. "Don't worry too much about me. I have no intention of staying longer than I must. Arthur simply decided that I was not adequately punished for my actions before he died, so he decided it was time to bring me back to serve a second penance."

"Arthur's dead?" That was surprising.

"So we assumed. He disappeared and never came back. I actually died many years later after serving my penance for my actions, but I suppose if Arthur never died then he would have never seen that." There was more there, more that he was not saying, and Alice did not press. He sounded more accepting than sad about it, like he was sure that he deserved it. But she didn't ask and she wasn't as interested anymore. There was no polite way for her to say so, so she stayed quiet and hoped he would stop talking.

Alice's attention went to a small collection of potions with stoppers in them, all looking very strange. Things floated inside them like the floral perfume bottles or photos of fancy teas, but she didn't know what these plants inside of them were. There was something unusual about them and their arrangement, all of them sitting on a pattern set into the table.

"He does care for you," Lance said after a few moments of silence. "Those are not my feelings, but his. I find you strange. But Arthur finds it more amusing to torment us both, I think."

Something was strange here. He wasn't like he was a moment ago or ever before. He was too nice, too sincere, and yet still too much unlike Lance. Arthur must be doing more than she realized in keeping him alive, and Alice didn't know what to make out of it. Not that it mattered. As soon as they found his heart, maybe this Lancelot would be gone and Lance could go back to normal. And they would never talk about this again.

Alice's attention soon went to another strange spot on the wall. The plants around them were loosening and receding back into the ground. Lance drifted across the room, gazing up longingly at the top of the bookshelf and looking out of breath and shaky. Still, he was standing, though possibly not for much longer.

Just a moment. She just wanted to look at this for a moment.

There was a mirror set in the middle of the wall along with several other pieces set in the walls around it, held in place by vines that looked like they had been very intentionally woven into their designs. There was something else in the branches, small stones and reflective pieces that looked almost alive, things made of metal and things that shone when she swayed back and forth. In the middle was a mirror with the vaguest impression of a face set in the other side, one that looked like it was not nearly strong enough to open its eyes just yet. It was strange and hypnotizing. She raised her hand, tempted to touch it and see just what it was. Her fingers hovered near the glass and the face, trying to decide if it was okay to touch.

She wouldn't, though. It wouldn't be polite. You did not touch another person's face, even if that person was a mirror, without asking first. It would be very rude.

"Alice!"

She snapped back around to see the sword clatter to the side of the room. Morgana stood between her and Lance, Lance poised like he was holding a sword in front of him and staring Morgana down. His face was flushed and he was sweating, his breathing rough. He was only barely keeping his feet and a moment later he collapsed to the side, his eyes flashing with terror to Alice, full of confusion and the realization that he was dying. Again.

Morgana didn't look happy about it either. Her hand waved at the bookshelf and Lance's heart came flying towards her, resting once more in her palm. There was something a little too real about it, possibly because this one was covered in blood that looked like it had begun to dry. She held it out to Alice, offering it to her to take.

Alice stared at it and then at her, not sure what to do with this. It looked like it wasn't a trap, but she also didn't know what Morgana was trying to do here.

Around them, the castle rumbled. Alice could hear the cracks as stone broke not too far away from them.

"Don't look at me like that, Alice," she said, not withdrawing her offer. "I have no love for men, but those boys have nothing to do with this, no matter how my brother might try to drag them in."

Alice looked from the heart to her, then back again. Finally, she took it. "Thank you."

Morgana nodded. "I won't be able to put it back myself. Find a way to return his heart and keep him away from here. I'll be dismantling this place soon and it won't be able to hurt anyone else."

That sent a chill of terror through Alice, but she didn't know why. The castle didn't do anything, but if that was all she was looking to do, she wasn't going to stop her. Without the castle, maybe the hole would heal up on its own and things would be fine. Still, she didn't stop the confusion from crossing her face. "Dismantling?" she asked. It seemed strange to take it apart brick by brick rather than just move it.

"This place is living on borrowed essence," Morgana told her. "Once I find the lynchpin keeping it together, I'll begin taking it apart and putting it back to the way it's meant to be. It has chosen someone. I do hope that isn't you."

"Me?" Alice asked, her mind racing to figure out what that meant. It sounded like a physical thing, not a person. "The Cheshire Cat was the one that chose me." She also had nothing to do with the castle.

"Then you won't have anything to worry about. At least, I hope not." Morgana smiled and pressed the heart into Alice's hands. "Go. We'll talk more later."

Alice took the heart and watched Morgana. When she did nothing to stop her, Alice picked up Lance with her free hand and draped one of his arms around her neck. Slowly she dragged him out of the room and tried to find her way out.

CHAPTER 26

Done Deal

"HELP!" ADRIANNA CALLED out into the throne room. Her arms were caught in the vines, the thorns piercing her skin and keeping her in place. "Please! Help me!"

The vines wouldn't stop growing. She couldn't stop them. Her heart thudded in her chest as she felt them continue to crawl up higher and higher. Around her, the brambles grew thicker and pulled more and more of the court into the mess. She didn't know how to make it stop, feeling them feeding off of her as they kept spreading. She didn't even feel drained as it kept happening as it used her desperation for them to stop.

She almost didn't want it to. It scared her how big and expansive it was getting, but it was drawing out the despair as it grew so large. She hadn't moved fast enough and Adam was hurt in front of her. He'd been pinned to the ground by the large spike, a spot of blood leaking out his back. He was barely moving on the ground in front of her.

Adam groaned in front of her, his back only slightly rising. It was too slow for him to be breathing. Much too slow. Adrianna wasn't even sure if that was him or just the vines making the ground tremble and making the sound. His head never rose and he didn't look at her. He said nothing.

He couldn't be dead. He couldn't.

"Help!"

The vines kept getting thicker, but they parted around Adrianna and Adam. At least they let her be with her brother, even if they had tangled up her arms. She needed to get free, to see if Adam was okay. She needed to know he was okay. She pulled desperately against them, pleading with the vines to let her go, to stop draining her of her fear and sadness and to let her go so she would know he was all right.

A voice broke through the sound of the trembling stonework around her and the vines came to a very abrupt halt. Adrianna, still yanking at the vines, fell forward as her arms came free. She dropped to the ground, looking around wide eyed with her tears making her vision blurry as she tried to see who had done it.

But she didn't have time. Adam.

"Thank you!" she called into the forest around her, still shaky as she crawled toward her brother. She was anxious as she got closer to him, hesitating to touch him. She didn't want him to be dead. She was scared that he really would be dead.

"Adam?" Adrianna asked, desperate to know he was okay. She hesitated before she reached out for his hand, only lightly tapping it before snapping her hand back. He couldn't be dead, but there was a lot of evidence to the contrary. He was lying impaled on a spike, directed straight through his heart and pinning him to the floor.

A groan escaped him and his hand curled into a fist.

Alive. He was alive.

"Adam!" She reached out again and held onto his hand. "Adam are you okay?"

Even in the groan and ragged breaths, she could hear his irritation at the question. Of course he wasn't all right. He was impaled and still possibly dying, even if it didn't look like he was leaking blood like he should be. He weakly held her hand, squeezing it as much as he could. That squeeze got tighter as he tried to move, the groan louder and shifting into agony before he settled back down into his spot on the ground.

"A Bandersnatch claw. Not how I would have done it, but I suppose it does the trick."

Adrianna looked up into the brambles around them and saw Arthur cutting his way clumsily through them with his sword. He was uncomfortable wielding it with his right, she could tell, and trying his best to use his other arm to push away what he could. He looked frustrated, his face drawn and jaw held tightly as he kept forcing himself on.

More importantly, he looked like he was alone.

There were a lot of other questions fighting to get out. What he was doing here? Where was Alice? Why wasn't he helping her? Where had Lance gone and if he was going to be okay without Arthur standing next to him? Something much more immediate slipped through her lips first.

"Can you help him?"

Arthur looked down at Adam and gave his leg a nudge. Adam groaned, gripping Adrianna's hand tighter. Adam communicated so much in groans anyway that even through the pain Adrianna could hear the irritation and anger.

"I'd be fine with leaving him like this," Arthur said, crouching down to look at his face. Adam shot back daggers, though Arthur didn't care. "He won't die from this. A Bandersnatch's claw, it doesn't kill unless you really want it to. If he's not dead yet, he won't be. It's just going to hurt a lot."

"Please Arthur. Please save him. Get him out. You can keep the claw," she offered. "It's magic, right?"

"Can't do much with a summoned one like this," Arthur said, flicking it. Adam squirmed at the bottom, biting back another groan of pain. "You have to either take it from the beast or have it willingly given. But," his attention turned back to Adrianna, thinking and a look passing over his face that Adrianna didn't trust, "there is something you could do for me."

Adam was already squeezing her hand and pulling her back, but she didn't care. "Anything," she told Arthur.

"No more playing coy," he told her. "Go out with me."

"Anything," Adrianna repeated. At the moment, it didn't matter. There was no ambiguity in what she was saying and she was barely listening, no matter how Adam tried to weakly protest under her. If it was to save her family, she would sacrifice whatever he asked of her.

Below her, Adam pulled his hand out of hers and threw himself to the side. Crying out in pain, he grabbed the tip of the claw protruding from his chest and pulled. His legs twitched and his screams echoed around them, drowning out Adrianna's pleas for him to stop, yanking it hard and pulling as much as he could out the front of his chest. Behind him and in his hands, the claw crumbled into dust, fluttering away into the vines and vanishing.

A desperate gasp for air came out of Adam as he struggled for breath. The hole in his chest started to close as soon as the claw was no longer holding it open and he curled in on himself as soon as he could, rolling onto his side and holding himself close. His hands clutched at the hole in his chest as he gasped for air, much too much like Lance had when he realized his heart was gone. Adam coughed and the look in his eyes was much more alive when he opened them again.

Relief flooded through Adrianna and she bent down to hug him, desperately happy that he wasn't dead too. This place was awful and losing someone to it, that was not something she thought could ever happen before a week ago. Now she had so nearly lost two. Had already maybe lost one. She couldn't stand to lose another. She knelt down to hug him, though he was not well enough for that and instead tried to help him get through his coughing and help him up.

"You aren't doing anything he tells you," Adam gasped out when he could speak again. He pushed himself up, putting himself between her and Arthur. "No way in hell I'm letting you— *Ah!*"

"It's okay," Adrianna said. "You don't have to move. We don't have to go anywhere yet."

"Where's Lance?" Adam asked, breathless and glaring up at Adrianna. He was shivering and still so shaken, but he was determined to get his answers, even if he couldn't move.

Adrianna put her hand on his arm, trying to keep him from trying to get up too fast. Still, Adam had a point. Wide eyed, she looked back at Arthur, watching for some look on his face that would tell her he was okay. That he was not too far. Maybe he was just outside or behind him.

Arthur was still for a moment, frowning. "He's with Alice."

"He's not with you?" Adrianna asked quietly. "Is he going to be okay?"

"That depends on how fast Alice can find us and get him back. I don't even know where to start looking for them, so he's in her hands now."

Adrianna stared at him, the tears once again stinging her eyes and her hands trembling. Adam was fine, she reminded herself. At least Adam would be okay. And Alice would be able to find them. She didn't want Lance to get hurt. She had to trust that Alice could bring him here before it was too late.

"Get me up," Adam groaned, pulling on Adrianna's arm. "Can't trust Alice. We're going to go meet them."

CHAPTER 27

If You Must

ALICE WAS GLAD when they found her. She was tired carrying Lance around, especially with how she had to balance him on her back with his heart cradled in her hands. She should have probably just gone to the smell of the forest that had come from the middle of the castle, but she was still very surprised to see the vines that had taken over so many of the halls and how high they stretched into the new, poorly made skylights. It might be high enough to cover the entire hole in Wonderland.

Alice was just glad for Arthur to be back. Lance jumped off her back and took his heart back, walking on his own to meet them in the hall and Alice took a seat where she stood to catch her breath. Lance was heavy. At least she had left his sword behind.

Adrianna's sleeves were tattered and there was a strange

tear in Adam's shirt that didn't appear in his coat. Something had happened to them. She wanted to ask, but she didn't know how, so she stayed quiet and where she was as she caught her breath and let them come to her.

"Should we leave?" Lance asked. "Do we still have to worry about guards with all this?"

"Not anymore," Adam said. His voice was strained and he walked hunched over now, looking short of breath. "Why the hell are you holding that. Alice, what are you doing? Get on with it."

Alice blinked and looked around again. Lance. Right. They had done all of this to get Lance's heart. She was supposed to put it back.

Just thinking about it was making her dizzy. She was glad she was sitting down.

"Right now?" she asked.

"*Yes*," Arthur said. "Get off your ass and get on it. Keeping a body alive is a lot harder than it should be."

Lance smiled and handed over his heart to Alice. She took it reluctantly. "Okay," she said quietly, trying to think. She still couldn't put hearts back, she knew she couldn't. She needed to think of something fast, but with so many people looking at her, she came up with nothing.

She felt her stomach knot and her breathing came out labored. The world around her lurched, but she kept her feet knowing that was only happening for her. She was going to have to show them she couldn't do it. She had no choice anymore.

"I'm sorry," she muttered quietly, not knowing if they heard or cared. She balanced the heart in one hand and looked at Lance. She stood in front of him, dreading what was about to happen and knowing there was nothing to do but try and fail. Her nerves, their eyes, none of it was working for her.

Her concentration fractured as soon as she began. She needed to get this done. There were so many people watching and expecting her to be able to do this, but the spell didn't want to be cast. It wasn't for her to do. It fought her as she tried to force herself to do it, to make the word come off of her trembling lips and with a voice that tried so hard to maintain control.

She could do this. Morgana had just handed the heart back. There had to be a way to break her spell if she pushed through it hard enough.

The more she fought it, the stronger the spell fought back. Her knees were weak and directions lost meaning. It was hard to stay standing when you lost track of where the ground was. Finding it took away her attention and the ground shifted and lurched around her. Alice stopped trying to stay upright and focused her concentration on trying to put the heart back. She wanted to. She could make herself before. But something was different here, something strange. Something wrong.

"Alice stop." The voice was calm and the hand gentle as it enveloped her. Lance was standing there, though it wasn't his eyes that were looking at her with such pity. He was holding her, keeping her from falling as she cupped his heart in her shaking hands. If not for him she would be on the ground, too dizzy and bleary-eyed to figure out what was going on. She was breathing heavily, heart still pulsing in her hand and trying to figure out what was going on.

Lance bent down to look her in the eye, studying her face and not really looking at her at all. She caught her breath and barely noticed she was being moved, the whole world spinning too much for her to notice, until he put her gently down against the wall with his heart still cupped in her hands.

"Cursed," he concluded, looking away. "For a while, from the looks of it. Looks like it was your..." Lance stopped as he looked at Arthur, a smile playing on his lips, knowing as he pulled himself back from whatever it was he was going to say. "Morgana, from the look of it."

Adrianna's voice came next, scared and mildly horrified. "She's really been cursed? Alice, did you know?"

"Of course she knew," Adam told her as Alice stayed quiet, trying to find where the floor was. He sounded bitter and didn't care that she was right there, head leaning back against the wall and staring up at the sky to try and regain her sense of balance. "The only thing she's good at and she can't even do it anymore."

"She *tried*," Adrianna snapped back at him. "Just let me think. There has to be something we can…"

Alice's ears filled with a very dense nothing, drowning out the world around her. The failure beat down on her and Alice could feel it in every thrum of Lance's damp heart. It beat so shallowly like it missed the body. Alice didn't know what to say to it either. She wasn't even sure that she knew how to put it back if she could put hearts back again. Neverland hearts didn't work like Wonderland hearts. There was no telling if she could figure out how to make Lance's heart go back in properly.

It was almost a shame that the world was starting to come back around her. She liked the moment of quiet.

"… do it."

"Addie!"

"I'll hold you to your word," Arthur said.

Arthur's lips were on hers before she knew what was happening. She didn't know when his hand had gotten hold of her face or why it would want to. There was no passion in it, more some combination of furious and mechanical. She was lifted up by her face off the ground, like he didn't want to bend over so much to kiss her, and she didn't dare move, too confused by what was happening until he finally let her go.

Alice dropped to the ground, barely keeping the heart from tumbling out of her hands as a fresh wave of dizziness overtook her and knocked her fully to the ground. Bleary-eyed, she watched as the world grew more colourful around her. She could see in sharp detail now as Adam charged forward, and she felt the vibration of the wall behind her as he shoved Arthur into it.

"Stop!" Adrianna looked panicked and watched in horror, pleading with Adam to stop. "Please, he wasn't going to—"

"He's a *creep*, Addie," Adam snapped back at her.

"Tell your brother he's not wanted here," Arthur told her.

"I'm not—"

"Please, Adam," Adrianna said, trying to grab him and pull him away. "It'll be okay. Please."

Adam almost didn't let go. Almost. He stared back at Arthur, looking like he might take another swing, but finally pulled himself out of Adrianna's arms and stormed down the hall. She could hear his swearing, quiet and under his breath, more colourful than before as he went around the corner.

Behind her, Lance helped Alice back up to her feet, taking his heart out of her hands. Her hands were slick with the red from it, though she had no napkin to wipe her hands off with. It was much more wet now, and she could see drops of blood pooling on the sides of it. She watched it curiously. It was still moving, still pulsing out here even. Somehow, that felt very unnatural. It was unlike any other heart she'd worked with.

Adrianna backed away entirely, her eyes wide and face paler than usual. She couldn't look away from it and she was very still, like if she didn't move the heart wouldn't notice her.

No, she wouldn't be able to get Adrianna to put hearts back for her.

"Well?" Arthur demanded. "I'm tired of this. Put it back."

"At least give her a minute," Adrianna snapped at him, her voice shaking. She sounded near tears, but Alice couldn't see her around Arthur. "What did you do to her?"

"The same thing I did to you," Arthur said, not turning around. Instead, he went over and grabbed Lance's heart from his hands and shoved it at Alice. "It's tiring keeping him alive. Go on."

Alice wasn't sure what was going on, head still woozy, but at least this she knew. For Lance, he was much more like those of Neverland. His heart was slippery in her hands, more difficult to hold with how much more strongly it was beating, but she could manage it much better.

As she concentrated, there was nothing stopping her from acting. "*Ábedecian geángang æþel innoÞ*," she said, acting more gingerly than she needed to. Everything came easily, like it had before. Maybe even more so. She could see just how all of it was meant to go, to how it was tied to his insides and how much it wanted to be back inside of him. It snapped back almost without needing the extra guidance from her, Lance lifting his shirt and the heart drifting back into the hole without a fuss.

It felt right. Putting the heart back, setting it in the hole, the magic felt more easy than anything else that had happened today, or in a while. Her mind was clear and the focus was finally there. Alice was finally able to do something that she was supposed to do. She had trouble figuring out how to get the Neverland hearts back in before, but she could see just how to make it fit this time and it was almost too easy. Maybe it was because of the notes, but she doubted it. Something else was making it fit.

Maybe it was because she was starting to feel like herself again.

In front of her, Lance's eyes came back to himself, as did the rest of him. He didn't hold himself as tall anymore, his head no longer balanced precariously on the topmost part of his neck. His stare was not so intense or earnest, his shoulders relaxing for the first time like he was no longer putting on a facade. Instead, Lance took in a breath and curling ever so slightly as he felt the heart settle back in his chest. The hole healed up mere moments later until it was like nothing had happened.

He took a second deeper breath, his eyes wide and looking around before he looked down at the shirt he was holding up. Alice drew her hand back and he quickly put it back down, face flushing even as he was feeling his chest and making sure that his heart was really sitting there where it was meant to be.

"Thanks," he said, almost breathless as he stared back at her. "I... um..." Lance looked lost, confused, and at a loss for words. He kept looking around, pressing his hand against his chest like he could feel his heart in there, and very carefully not looking at Arthur.

"You're welcome," Alice said. Might as well be polite while he appeared to be having a crisis.

Adrianna threw her arms around him, looking like she was about to cry. Alice stepped away, away from Arthur and whatever he might try to grab her for next and away from the Cases and their reunion. She saw Adam lingering just around the corner and nodded for him to go join his sister in welcoming his brother back to himself. Glaring around the corner at Arthur, he still went to join them.

Taking another breath, Alice realized just how tired she was. She reached out into nothing and grabbed the mirror from the Queen's room of hearts. When she tried to pull it back, it resisted. Finally, she felt something snap as she yanked it hard, pulling it out of the air in front of her.

"We can head back whenever you're ready," Alice said, displaying the mirror now open to their dorm room once more. "I do hope you will be ready soon."

"You're okay," Adrianna muttered into Lance's shoulder, holding him hard and not noticing how Arthur was looming over them. "You're back."

Lance said something back to her, holding her tight in response, something too quiet for Alice to hear.

Behind them, Arthur checked his wrist and made his way toward the mirror. Irritation and annoyance marked his face and he looked like his patience was finally running out. He held up his hand and waited only a moment before he made a gesture, a look of concentration crossing his face as it looked like he yanked something out of the air toward Lance.

"What?" Adrianna asked, her voice louder and filled with disbelief.

Lance let go of Adrianna, her eyes wide and scared again as he separated himself from her. She didn't know what was happening, but Alice watched as Arthur looked pleased with himself. Watched as regret and sadness crossed over Lance's face, of a resigned fate as something completely different overtook it a moment later and he got to his feet, going to Arthur's side.

"I'm not done with him yet," Arthur said, Lance getting up and going to Arthur's side, looking like someone who was very much not Lance. That lopsided grin and mischief looked much more plastic now than it had before, and he was holding himself much too tightly for Alice to believe he was doing so too willingly.

"See you around, sis," he said, heading through the mirror and leaving his sister behind, staring after him as he left.

"Don't forget," Arthur told Adrianna, a smile and mischievous look on his face as he leaned back in the room. "You're bound to it now. But don't worry. I'll make you come to me willingly soon enough."

Adrianna watched as they left, jaw held tight and letting out an angry breath. Alice had never seen her angry before. "It's okay," she said, her demeanour softening as she turned to look at Alice. "I'll help you get everything settled with Wonderland. And once that's done, we'll never have to deal with any of this ever again. Let's go home."

CHAPTER 28

Points of Contention

THERE WAS A time that Adrianna would have been happy that finals were over for the year, but she already missed the distraction. Finals were so much easier this year than ever before, which was good given that she was not sleeping well. Every time she dozed off, she could see the Queen of Hearts with that terrible claw, saw Adam on the ground with a spike out his back, saw Lance holding his own beating heart. It still itched where the thorns bit into her skin and she could feel them feeding off of her sadness and desperation as they grew around her.

At least Lance was alive. It was a small comfort, but comfort still. Inside there somewhere, her brother was still alive, even if there was something else using his body right now. She could only hope that Arthur wouldn't do anything to hurt him.

Well, if she did what he wanted...

"Hey Addie, you okay in there?" She rubbed at a tired eye and looked around to the mostly empty common room. Since the theater rooms were full, they grabbed a couple couches and opted to make their own movie marathon without the big screen to celebrate the end of finals. Rob went through his laptop to find something for them to watch, Sarah lingering over his shoulder making suggestions. Across from her, she could see Adam and Heather had finally moved past flirting and properly into being a couple, their hands entwined and Heather resting back against him as her free hand tapped on her phone.

"Sorry," she said. "I haven't been sleeping much."

"Me neither," Heather said with a groan. "But it's over now. Almost."

"Almost?"

"Don't get her started," Adam warned her.

"Addie loves hearing about Council stuff."

"*No one* loves hearing about Council stuff."

She elbowed him hard in the ribs and, though Adam laughed, Adrianna couldn't help but shuffle a little away. The image of him on the ground pulling that spike out of his chest was still too fresh. He insisted that it was better and there was nothing to worry about, but Adrianna wished he would take it easy. He'd almost died and getting an elbow to the ribs surely wasn't helping.

Not that Heather knew that. Or that she could tell her. Adrianna didn't know how to handle all these secrets. She wished Alice were here, but she and Kevin had one last shift at the Library to fulfill for the semester. Adam was of no help, going back to normal and looking like it hadn't affected him at all. Like he wasn't having nightmares from everything.

But it was Adam. He probably wasn't.

"You look really tired, Addie," Heather said. "You sure you're okay?"

"Yeah, I…" Adrianna stifled a yawn. She didn't think she was that sleepy, but maybe she was. "Maybe I'll just go take a nap for a bit? I'll join you guys for dinner."

"I'll help you up," Adam said, disentangling himself from Heather. He trailed behind Adrianna, saying nothing as he walked behind her up the stairs.

She felt her phone vibrate in her pocket and looked at it, seeing a message from Sarah waiting for her. She dismissed it for now, not even sure what she would want. She glanced back, but Sarah and Rob looked like they were in deep discussions about what they should be watching.

When they got to her room, Adam gently shut the door behind them. "Nightmares?"

"You almost *died*," Adrianna reminded him. "*Lance was dead*. How am I supposed to sleep after that?"

"No one's dead. That's how."

"That doesn't—"

"And so long as Alice keeps doing what she's supposed to, no one *will* die. Nothing to keep you up at night."

"What do you have against Alice?"

"You know that already," Adam told her. "After what you did, I'm surprised you're still pretending you like her."

"*Me?* I didn't—"

"You didn't what?" Adam asked, staying on his face and seeming to grow taller. His eyes were cold more than they were curious and something in his voice made her go very quiet. It wasn't amusement, much too dark for that, but she didn't know that she had heard this kind of control before. "You didn't wait until she was half conscious and tell a guy you *know* is a creep to make out with her? Didn't I see that, Addie? And you didn't try to tell me that I should just let it happen?"

"I… I didn't…" She could feel the tears stinging her eyes at the accusation. It was cruel to put it that way. He was ignoring what was happening on purpose, looking for a reason to turn this into an argument. "I had to!" She tried to tell him. "She was cursed! And Lance was… He was…"

But her words didn't move Adam. His feet took a step back at the sight of the tears on her face, but he was still disapproving behind the discomfort of seeing her cry. She didn't even know why she was crying. She had done nothing wrong, but still the tears kept coming. She didn't want to say yes to Arthur. She didn't want to go out with him. But she didn't want her brother dead either. And she didn't want her friend to be cursed. It was the only way.

"I didn't want to!" she tried to implore him. She needed him to understand, but the heat in her chest was already rising to her throat and she was yelling before she could stop herself. "I had to do it! You don't understand, I had to!"

"If you wanted someone to be sympathetic, you would have been better with Lance."

"Fine!" Adrianna snapped at him. "*Ábedecian Lance Michael Case hércyme...*"

Adam's eyes flew wide, watching as his sister tearfully called for another brother. He didn't move, frozen as he watched his sister drop to the floor, her fingers doing nothing to hide the racking sobs that had overtaken her.

Adrianna knew she had done the right thing. Alice needed the curse broken. Lance needed his heart back. She was the only one who would have to suffer by fulfilling her side of the agreement. She was the one who now had to go out with

Arthur, and even that was a small price to have her brother alive. Alice had said nothing after it happened, and she looked happier now that the curse was gone.

"You know he's not Lance anymore, right?" Adam asked quietly.

Adrianna looked up at him. The tears hadn't stopped, but she still wiped them away so she could see him clearly, to see if she could spot a reason he was so cruel. There was nothing there, his face as blank as his voice. He knew he was right and so did Adrianna.

"Wonderland made you so cruel," she told him, the words coming out between deep breaths. "I wish it were gone."

"Don't blame Wonderland. He's always been like that."

Adrianna and Adam snapped back to the door. Neither of them had heard it open, but Lance was now leaning in the doorway. He offered half a smile before taking a deep breath and letting his shoulders sag. "Don't you even try," he added to Adam. "We both know you've always been a dick. More than Matt ever was."

Adrianna got to her feet and threw her arms around him, hugging him tight and sobbing into his shoulder. He felt so warm when he hugged her back, so much like himself again. For this moment, she could let herself forget that she didn't really save him.

"You'll be okay," he told her.

"Don't lie to her," Adam snapped. "How did you get free? I thought Arthur had you on a leash."

"We'll have time later. What did you do?"

"Why do you think it's me?"

There was quiet except for Adrianna's calming sobs. She kept her face in Lance's shoulder and tried to bring herself together. It was really him. That's what Adam said. That this was really Lance. That she didn't fail, that she hadn't done all this for nothing. That he was really back.

"Wonderland is hard," Lance said gently. "Best not to get involved if you can help it."

"He said I shouldn't have helped her."

"I said she shouldn't have told the creep who gets off making out with unconscious chicks to go make out with Alice while she was practically unconscious."

"Have you apologized?" Lance asked.

Adrianna hesitated. She didn't know why everyone was getting mad at her about this. She had done the right thing. She broke the curse on Alice and got Lance his heart back. The only way to do either of those things was to agree to a date with Arthur. She was sure Alice would have agreed with her that it was necessary. She hadn't even mentioned it afterwards.

"She wasn't mad," Adrianna offered weakly.

"Addie," Lance told her gently. "Apologize. She wouldn't have done that to you. And talk to her."

Adam let out a grunt at that. "What's she going to do?"

"She's been dealing with Wonderland longer than any of us," Lance told him firmly before turning his attention back to Adrianna. "Talking about it will help. And I'll be around all summer if you need it."

"What about now?" Adam asked.

"Now I can feel Arthur looking for me," he said. "And if I stay here much longer, all of this is going away. And you'll have to deal with Arthur. I don't think that's what you need right now." He pulled himself away from Adrianna and backed into the door. "You'll have me for the summer. Talk to Alice. See you in a bit."

Adrianna stared after him, her arms wrapping around herself. She hated this. She hated all of this. Everything that Wonderland touched turned terrible and she wished they could all be done with it. She didn't know what she had ever seen in the place. There was a time she thought it was a magical and amazing world that couldn't possibly be as bad as Alice told her. And she had been right. It was worse.

"You should also tell Lance you killed the Queen of Hearts," Adam told her.

Adrianna shot a glare back at him, already feeling the guilt and fear welling up inside her again. She didn't know how Alice had done this for so many years. What Wonderland had made her do.

Lance was right. Alice had been there longer than anyone. She should really talk to Alice when she got back.

Her phone vibrated in her pocket and she picked it up. More messages from Sarah. Adrianna opened it this time, catching up on the few that she'd missed.

Sarah

You look like you could use book club

You are officially invited

In January

Sarah

Kevin says Alice didn't make it to library

You know where she is?

CHAPTER 29

Caterpillar's Decree

THE CASTLE WAS quiet. It wasn't empty, but Alice got the distinct feeling that she shouldn't be wandering around here. That it wasn't safe. That there was still a sorceress who was once her best friend's stepmother in the castle who wanted to talk to her.

But now there were very few people walking through the castle. Shadows moved showing that people were there, but none tried to come for her. For now, no one knew she was there. If she was fast, she wouldn't be caught. She just needed to not get too distracted. She just needed to see one thing.

Alice entered the throne room now so densely covered in vines that she didn't know how she would walk in. Not until she saw a large hole in the vines, like someone had barrelled right through to the middle. Someone had cleared the way for her, someone who was a little too short. Alice ducked and moved slowly toward the throne.

Adam was the one that told her that the Queen of Hearts was dead now. He wouldn't say how, only that Alice could see her for herself. In the middle of the throne room, the Queen was supposed to be a statue. Someone else had done what she was supposed to do and he had sounded so smug about it.

At no time did Alice think she was supposed to kill the Queen of Hearts. She had done such terrible things, had terrorized and changed Wonderland, but killing people wasn't what you did in Wonderland. Some tried, but it wasn't ever supposed to really happen. The Queen of Hearts had done all this much because her husband had died and she was driven mad because of a magic book. She wouldn't get a happy ending for everything she'd done, but it still felt like the wrong end for her.

Alice made it to the end of the path and the dome where she could stand up. There were dots of blood on the ground by a series of fallen thorns. She'd seen the scratches on Adrianna's arms and she'd said something about not being able to control the vines, but Alice wondered now if she should have asked more. She had looked so uncomfortable that she had left her alone.

In front of her, there was an empty space. Alice could tell that there was supposed to be something there, the vines curled around in the shape of a statue that might have been the Queen of Hearts, but there was no statue.

"Did she escape?" Alice asked. She already knew she had company before even the fluffy tip of his purple tail appeared. She didn't know when he had gotten back, but she wasn't surprised that he was now that the battle was over.

"She is a statue of a different colour now," the Cheshire Cat told her.

"Does this mean it's over?" Alice kept staring at the space, not sure what to make of any of this. She hadn't done this. After everything, it didn't feel complete. She didn't know why, but it felt like she was supposed to defeat the wicked queen and bring peace to Wonderland. Maybe choose a successor and allow the White King his turn after the Queen of Hearts had taken far too long with Wonderland. It didn't feel complete to have someone else defeat her.

Maybe she'd been reading too many books. Real life didn't wrap up so nicely. Not even in Wonderland

The Cheshire Cat crawled across her shoulders, putting his weight down on her. She lurched forward, but kept her balance as he got comfortable. "If you consider a job complete when you've left holes all over the place, then we have brought in the wrong person. Holes in the ceiling, holes in the people, holes in the sky. Are you so ready to be done?"

Alice said nothing for a long time. She knew she should

say yes. The right answer would be to say yes, that she was done and going back to her real life now. She had to go back, to see her friends one last time before she went home to her father. She should be excited about the holidays and whatever it was her father had planned. The solitude and knowing that she would be watched carefully every waking moment during it.

She should be happy she was almost done. All that was left was to put the hearts back now. Nothing would take them back anymore. She had time to put everything back, to figure out how to close the hole and finish the rest. "I can't come back until after the break to fix any of that."

It was Cat's turn to have a strange silence. "You are too often the topic of conversation, Alice," he said. "Even when you are barely here, you leave a shadow that cannot speak for herself. It has become a problem."

"I'll be here more after the break," Alice said. "I cannot be held responsible for how often other people talk about me when I'm not here. I would question their manners, though. I should think if I'm the one being talked about, I should be there."

"Agreed," Cat said. "The Hatter has never thrown a good party, but he is throwing a very good argument and you are the main subject."

Alice let out a sigh. "All right," she said. "Where are they?"

"They are where they are," Cat said, vanishing. "You should perhaps look there first."

THE PARTY HAD moved to under the large weeping willow, the Jabberwocky still fast asleep atop the cushion that appeared to be made just for him. The party beneath it was indeed not so much a party as it was an argument. Loud voices were talking over one another, none of them in a jovial tone and all of them fighting to be heard over the other. Others stayed very quiet, spectating as Tiger Lily and the Mad Hatter ranted back and forth at one another.

Alice found a seat by the empty cup of sugar the Dormouse refused to call his bed. The cup jostled a little as she brought herself to the table and she was quick to quietly apologize for the interruption. He barely registered what was happening, once more protesting that he was indeed awake and Alice could let the argument about her rage around her while she waited her turn at the head of the table.

"It is hardly polite to make a decision like this without so much as a consult!" Hatter scolded Tiger Lily across the table.

Alice took a cup of tea off the table and one of the Mad Hatter's heartless helpers was quick to fill it for her so she could take a sip. Surprisingly, it was pleasant and tasted faintly of rose.

"Polite isn't important! It isn't *safe* if she comes here again! We will all die if Alice is caught, and I will not permit that."

"That is for Wonderland to decide, not you! Wonderland will choose who belongs here and who may only be visiting for a time. I should remind you both that you have been guests, and not terribly good ones at that."

"I should say I've been a perfectly fine guest," Caterpillar intoned through the smoke.

"I should say that you have as well, my apologies," Hatter told him, calming almost immediately. "This is still well outside of what a guest should be deciding. You may stay, but you may not decide who may enter and leave. That is for whoever has the keys to determine. You cannot simply steal someone's keys and decide they no longer live there."

"Removing the keys is better than letting the key holder bring in fire to burn the house down."

"The fire is being brought in by your companion, I believe," Hatter told him darkly. "As well as all the intent to light it."

Cat appeared around the back of Alice's chair and let out a loud cough. Alice wasn't sure when he got there, but his fur was on end and he let out a low growl with every word. "Perhaps you would like to speak to the kindling yourself."

"Alice of Wonderland!" Tiger Lily looked distinctly

uncomfortable, flushing and not quite meeting her eyes as Alice put down her cup. "When did you arrive?"

"Very rude to not announce yourself," Hatter agreed.

"You were having such a good argument that I didn't want to interrupt. I am very curious what you are saying about me when you think I am not there."

"It is possible that politeness is also rudeness." He was flustered, but managed to pull himself together to look at her. "I'm afraid these two have been making some choices on behalf of everyone without even so much as a consult! I don't want to seem unwelcoming to guests, but it's quite out of line to assume they can make decisions without talking to anyone else about it."

"It needed to be done," Tiger Lily told him firmly. She looked at Alice. "I am sorry, Alice of Wonderland. We want only to protect this place and this was the only way."

"I don't know what you did," Alice told them. "But if it's to help—"

"*Hardly!*" Hatter exclaimed, slamming his hands down on the table. "Neverland is changing, perhaps. *I* think it looks about as much as a mangy muddle as it has ever been. Terrible place, always too dark. It's no wonder no one knows how to so much as knock! Thinking that the people of Wonderland will suddenly also forget their manners just because there's a new queen in the castle presupposes far too much about us."

"Well, I suppose if they're going to go about this again," Cat said, curling around her shoulders and resting his face by her ear. "The circle will eventually become a straight line, but it takes so much effort. You are hearing the long of it, but the short is that your middle wish has been revoked and you may no longer come to Wonderland through the mirrors."

Cat sounded dismissive about it, but the words were echoing in her ears. She couldn't come back. Her access to the mirrors, it was gone. It didn't sound real. She didn't know what they meant about her middle wish or what that might have to do with anything. Thoughts ran around in circles, trying to figure out what was wrong with what they were saying. It couldn't be real. Wonderland needed her, didn't it?

"But that's how I got here," Alice said weakly, drawing their eyes. "Are you sure you did anything?"

It went quiet around the table, the argument coming to a very abrupt halt to hear her. It stretched on for moments that each felt too long.

"One last time," Caterpillar told her. "Only polite to tell you that you would not be allowed back. The Bandersnatch was most gracious about that."

Of course. Alice deflated in her seat. She had sent the

Bandersnatch here and of course they would figure out how to use him. Why they would, she still didn't understand, but it also didn't matter. They were locking her out. They didn't want her here anymore and they made sure she couldn't come back. "Is that where the Queen of Hearts went?" she asked. "A statue of a different colour."

Tiger Lily looked guilty as she sat down at the table. The Caterpillar did not, puffing on his hookah and watching her without regrets. Only Hatter stepped up and around her, taking off his hat with a flourish and bowing to present it to her.

"So that you may remember us by something," he told her. "The actions of two have overridden the wishes of many. Though I do hope you return one day to return it. It is the Jabberwocky's favourite. I fear I may fall out of his favour if I am apart from it for too long."

"Then you will fall out of favour with the beast," Caterpillar told him.

"Thank you," she said, putting it on. She felt hollow as he held out his hand. It didn't matter that he didn't want her gone, she was gone nonetheless. She took it and shook it before she turned away. "I'll be gone now."

As she walked aimlessly through Wonderland in search of a mirror, Cat appeared beside her and followed her with every step. "Ridiculous, before you ask," he said. "No understanding of how this works. But they don't need to know that you've never needed a mirror to return. And it will be so nice to have those to myself again. Very rude of you to take them from me for so long."

The hat felt heavy on her head and her mind was turning in more circles than her path. Without the mirrors, she wasn't going to be able to return. And without her, Wonderland would get no worse or better. It would deal with itself, fight its own battles without her, survive. It would be better without her and she could go back to her own life.

And she should be happy about that.

"Careful, Alice," he warned her, amusement dripping through his words as they made it to the mirror. "Wouldn't want to cause another flood."

"Goodbye Cat," Alice said. She appeared in front of a mirror in the middle of the ruins of the Duchess' castle. On the other side, she could see her dorm. Her packed bags and Adrianna's. It was time for her to go.

"You think you'll be rid of me so easily," he said. "Back to your large cage? The one that watches you and makes you so miserable and a father who thinks he is a king over all he sees?"

Alice shrugged. That's what she was supposed to want. Back home to a father that cared about her enough to keep an eye on her. Back to rules that were set for her own good. She had done it before and she would do it again. "It's my home," she said. "Where else would I go?"

About the Author

TANYA LISLE IS a novelist from Metro Vancouver, British Columbia, who has series littered across genres from supernatural horror to young adult fantasy. She began writing in elementary school, when she started turning homework assignments into short stories and continued this trend well into university. While attending Simon Fraser University, she developed an appreciation for public domain crossovers and cross-platform narratives. She has a shelf full of notebooks with more story ideas than pens lost to the depths of her bag. Now she writes incessantly in hopes of finishing all of them.

Thankfully, her cat, Remy, has figured out how to shut off Tanya's computer when she needs to take a break.